MIKE LOW spent most of his Royce plc where he was involve engines for the Civil aerospa sectors. Mike also spent so manufacture of other Rolls-Royce power plants for use in the Marine and Nuclear divisions.

In 2013 Mike published his first book *The Bleedin' Obvious Way to Improve Quality in Your Business*. His second, *Saviour of the Free World*, the story of the Rolls-Royce Merlin aero engine, followed in 2015. *The Voyage of An Luchog* is his first novel.

Mike is married and lives in Somerset. To find out more about Mike, visit his website at: www.mikelow.co.uk.

THE
VOYAGE
OF AN LUCHOG

MIKE LOW

SilverWood

Published in 2017 by SilverWood Books

SilverWood Books Ltd
14 Small Street, Bristol, BS1 1DE, United Kingdom
www.silverwoodbooks.co.uk

Copyright © Mike Low 2017

The right of Mike Low to be identified as the author of this work
has been asserted in accordance with the Copyright,
Designs and Patents Act 1988 Sections 77 and 78.

All rights reserved. No part of this publication may be reproduced,
stored in a retrieval system, or transmitted in any form or by
any means, electronic, mechanical, photocopying, recording or
otherwise, without prior permission of the copyright holder.

This is a work of fiction. Names, characters, places and incidents
either are products of the author's imagination or are used
fictitiously. Any resemblance to actual events or locales or
persons, living or dead, is entirely coincidental.

ISBN 978-1-78132-656-5

British Library Cataloguing in Publication Data
A CIP catalogue record for this book is available
from the British Library

Page design and typesetting by SilverWood Books
Printed on responsibly sourced paper

Chapter 1

'Now then, Mr Keystone, I'm sure we can come to some arrangement whereby you wouldn't become completely penniless.'

'How? In what way? By calling in the loan you are effectively destroying my Ascalon charity! It has taken years to set up and has saved hundreds of destitute and homeless people from penury! Why are you doing this? Your representatives gave me a clear understanding that the loan would not need to be repaid for three years. I believed them. Now, after just three months, your bank is demanding full repayment. You have misled me and my charity. Why?'

'Now, Mr Keystone. I'm sure we don't want any harsh words at this time. But you were hardly misled. You were given a very good interest rate – less than three per cent on your loan – and you were told that there was the possibility that the loan would be called in early. Surely you read the small print in the contract? Come, let us look at what disposable assets you have and see if something can be arranged to help the situation.'

Clark looked long and hard at the man sitting in front of him, on the opposite side of his large mahogany desk.

As desks go it was gargantuan. It could have doubled as a table-tennis table. Clark enjoyed being behind it, not least because it had the effect of intimidating those who had to talk to him across its polished width. Keystone was trapped, thought Clark. What could the fool do? The Ascalon charity, built up over the last ten years by him and his wife, with the aim of helping the homeless riff-raff on the streets of Bristol, was doomed. Clark knew that the man opposite had mortgaged his home and sought loans to provide funds to promote its work, in addition to working regularly at the many reception centres set up in Bristol and the surrounding area. Keystone's position was utterly hopeless. The hard and calculating Rupert Pelham Clark was about to triumph yet again. Keystone looked resigned and said, 'What do you suggest?'

'Let's see what can be done. Surely you and your family have enough assets to pay off your loan? You must understand I run a business, Mr Keystone, and I cannot allow that to suffer just to help out some poor unfortunates who can't – or won't – work. I have been generous in allowing you three months to find the means to pay off the loan, but there comes a time when no business can wait forever, and that time is now.'

Clark knew that the finality of his 'now' would echo around the office and bounce repeatedly off the walls and windows into John Keystone's ears. Oh, how he enjoyed seeing him suffer!

Rupert Clark was relishing watching Keystone become ever more resigned to his fate. What was it to him? Had he not given the charity an opportunity to pay off the huge loan it had undertaken? Was he supposed to let his own interests suffer just because this fool, now sitting in front of him, wanted to offer assistance to the lazy, idle riff-raff polluting the streets of Bristol? No way! No! Now was the time to collect and, with the plan he had in mind, make himself another fortune if he could force Keystone into the right corner.

'My wife and I have some small savings. I will cash them and they will help.'

'How much?'

'I'm not sure. Probably around twenty-five thousand pounds.'

'But Mr Keystone, you and your charity owe my bank more than four hundred thousand pounds. We have to have the full amount by the end of this month or else I must call in the receiver.'

'Surely you can give us one more month, just one more?'

'No, I cannot. What assets do you have?'

The utter hopelessness of his predicament now loomed spectre-like in John Keystone's mind. The only way to raise the large amount of money required would be to sell the family home in Ireland along with any or all of their furniture, paintings and other contents. He and his wife would have to live permanently in the small, one-bedroomed flat they rented in Bristol, which they used when they were there running their charity.

'I will have to sell the family home in Ireland and all its contents to raise anything like that amount!'

'So be it then. And the contents. What are they? Is there anything of value among them? And how long will it take to sell your home – can it be realised within the next two weeks? My bank needs this loan repaid soon in order to continue in business.'

Clark knew that his last statement was a blatant lie. The RPC Bank was well able to continue in business without repayment of Keystone's loan. He had his own reasons for calling it in. He was planning to make many more millions from the predicament faced by the man in front of him. He knew Keystone had no alternative. The pathetic do-gooder had only himself to blame. The loan must be paid or there would be a court case and seizure of Keystone's home and assets. The ensuing bad publicity would mean the death-knell of the Ascalon charity.

Keystone gazed out of the office window, his eyes traversing the London skyline, taking in the immensity of the towering Shard and onwards upriver towards St Paul's Cathedral. He thought of the millions of people under his gaze. If only he had £1 from each of them all would be saved! But that, of course, was not to be. At least if he could get the RPC Bank off his back by selling his home, appeals could be made to others to help keep the charity going.

'I'd better instruct an estate agent immediately to place the house on the market at an attractive price. The contents can be sold at auction, but that will take some time to arrange. May I use your phone to set this all in motion?'

'Of course. Help yourself.' Clark pushed one of the phones on his desk towards Keystone, who proceeded to call an estate agent in Dungloe, County Donegal. Clark got up from his chair and walked out of the office. His plan was going exactly as he had hoped. He left Keystone alone in his office to stew for a while. He knew what would be going through his mind. I bet he's wishing right now he'd never let himself be talked into coming to me for a loan, thought Clark.

After instructing the estate agent, Keystone, alone in the empty office, pondered his fate. He knew his wife, Rita, would understand this predicament. He'd told her exactly what was likely to happen before he left Bristol to travel to London for this fateful meeting. She would support him, though they would be in considerably reduced circumstances for the foreseeable future. The Ascalon charity? Well, almost the end, he thought, though appeals to kindly donors and others may save it from folding – time would tell. If only he had not been so persuasively advised to go to the RPC Bank. If only he had not taken notice of those who suggested this bank as an organisation who would support the charity with a sizeable loan at short notice, and at a very good interest rate, to help them get through an awkward situation and save a number of families who had hit very hard times. If only.

Keystone looked up as Clark re-entered the office and said, 'Now, Mr Keystone. What about your assets? What possessions have you got stashed away in that home of yours? Is there anything of value?'

'No. Nothing really. Just furniture and a couple of paintings, that's all. I will sell them at auction, though as I've already said, that may take some time to set in motion.'

'Perhaps I can help you there. The paintings, what are they and who are the artists?'

'I don't know really. They just came with the house and have been there ever since we bought the place twelve years ago. They look quite old.'

'Mmmm. Doesn't sound too good. Have you any photos of them?'

'Yes, actually. They are in my briefcase. I brought them with me just in case they might be worth something.' He opened his briefcase and, after rummaging around for a short while, produced some photos.

'Here you are,' he said, handing the photos to Clark.

One photo showed a seascape, probably a view near Keystone's house on Aranmore, Co Donegal. The other was a picture of a young lady in fine eighteenth-century clothes, gazing out of the painting. Clark hid his excitement at seeing the pictures.

'Well, they look interesting enough. Might be worth a few thousand I suppose. Say £3,000 for the pair.'

'£3,000 for the pair!' exclaimed Keystone. 'But they might be worth a lot more!'

'Really Mr Keystone. Can't you see I'm trying to help you out? I can hardly wait until you have arranged a valuation and then an auction. Time is running out for you. You have a firm offer on the table. Make up your mind.'

Clark had John Keystone in a corner that would appear to be getting tighter by the minute. Keystone realised there was no way out and this seemed like a quick way of raising some cash.

'Very well. £3,000 it is. And the estate agent told me over the phone that he has a number of people interested in buying property on Aranmore. He intends to show them my home and hopes to get an early sale, especially at the low selling price.'

'Good. Let's hope there is a quick sale. I suggest we meet again in a week and discuss progress. In the meantime,

Mr Keystone, I will arrange to have those two paintings removed from your house, if you don't mind.'

'All right,' said Keystone. He did not appear to notice the apparent haste with which Clark wanted the paintings removed and brought under his own control. Clark guessed that right now the other's mind was too full of extra details to worry about two paintings that he never seemed to have been much interested in anyway.

'Right. Then I'll bid you good day.'

Keystone mumbled a goodbye, turned and left the office.

Later that evening, in their Bristol flat, John told Rita what had happened in London.

'And the paintings. You sold him the paintings?' she asked with just a suggestion of loss in her voice.

'Really had no choice. At least it gives us a start to pay off the loan. He had me over a barrel. I just wanted to avoid bad publicity or a court case – or both. I am sorry it's come to this, darling. I'll work really hard to get us and the charity back on track, but we must get this man off our backs – we really must. Oh how I wish we'd never followed the advice from those people and gone to that bank for the loan.'

'And our house – how much can we expect to get and will it pay off the loan?'

'Well, the estate agent expects it to realise €400,000, which, together with our savings and the bits and pieces from selling the contents and the paintings, should pay off the bulk of the loan.'

Rita loved her husband dearly. She hated to see him having to go to such lengths to save all that they had worked for during the last ten years. She suppressed the tears that were beginning to well up. They would not help the predicament they were now in.

'OK, sweetheart, I understand. We will get through this together. I love you.'

John Keystone reached out to his wife and hugged and kissed her in love and appreciation.

'You truly are the most wonderfully supportive wife any man could wish for. Thank you, darling.'

They both knew that the future was going to be a struggle, but were determined to face it together and win through somehow.

John Keystone had grown up and been to school in Bristol. He knew the city very well and had many relatives living in and around its neighbourhoods. When he had left school he managed to get a place at Plymouth University studying chemistry, and it was there that he had met Rita. They had married soon after leaving university. Rita was from Ireland and they had both decided, some years previously, to live there, somewhere peaceful and picturesque. She had been a successful actress, appearing on stage and in films, and had made a very good living from it. Though now retired from acting, Rita loved being involved with charity work. Her acting success had produced a sizeable fortune that, together with John's earnings from working for a major pharmaceutical company, helped them to buy their house on Aranmore and to start up their charity.

They loved being together. The world was a wonderful place when they shared each other's company. When in Bristol they spent their time helping the many volunteers to run their charity and they really enjoyed being a key part of its success in helping others. They were determined to overcome the huge setback caused by the RPC Bank and win through somehow.

Chapter 2

Back in London Rupert Clark was savouring the soon-to-be-realised success of his plan. He had already despatched his aide, Mr Smee, to Ireland with instructions to secure the paintings from the Keystone house and ensure their delivery to his own home in Tralee. He had also made arrangements for the paintings to be transported by sea rather than by road. The distance by sea from Aranmore to Tralee was no more than 300 nautical miles, which should, he calculated, take no longer than just a day and a half. He wanted the paintings in his house safely and in a reasonable time, and he had reasons why sending them by road would not necessarily be the safest thing to do. Clark knew that he was not the only one who believed that one of the paintings might be worth a great deal of money. The art expert hired by him to view that particular painting had passed on his opinion, for a price, to someone he knew would stop at nothing to get hold of the painting. Clark had found out about this betrayal of confidence through a spy who had been privy to the conversation between the art expert and Hugh Jayce, who was an enemy of Clark's following a joint business deal, years ago, that had made Clark millions and Jayce nothing. Jayce had never forgiven

Clark for his skulduggery in the deal, and had vowed to get even one day.

Clark also knew of a few people who would be very interested in purchasing the painting if it proved to be an Old Master, and he did not want these very rich potential buyers to be kept waiting.

One of the telephones on Clark's desk rang. Few people knew the number, only very close business contacts and some family members. Most calls to him were channelled through his secretary, Mabel. He lifted the receiver.

'Hello, Rupert. Is that you?' It was Clark's long-suffering wife, Holly.

'Yes, of course it's me. What on earth do you want at this time? You know I'm very busy.'

'Yes dear, I know. But I just had to let you know that Hillary has just gone to hospital and is likely to give birth today. We could be grandparents before midnight. Don't you think that's worth celebrating?'

'Perhaps, but not now. Is there anything else?'

'No, dear. I do wish you'd be a little more interested. Hillary is our daughter, after all.'

'Yes, yes. Now I really must go.'

'But what time will you be home tonight? We must go and visit Hillary.'

'I will not be home this evening. I have an important client coming for a business meeting later on. I will let you know tomorrow when I shall be home. I have to go now.'

The receiver was quickly returned to its holder. Clark had little time for Holly. He had long grown tired of her and, as he saw it, her interfering ways. She was a dutiful wife who took great care of and interest in their two children,

Hillary and Hugh, and was seemingly endlessly tolerant of her husband and his bad temper and indifference towards her. Most women in such a one-sided relationship would have left their marriage long ago.

Satisfied that his wife would not be bothering him again today, he picked up the other phone on his desk and said, 'Mabel, get me Smee as soon as you can.'

'Yes, Mr Clark. Right away.'

Mabel had long become hardened to the abrasive, tactless and rude ways of her boss and was occasionally a witness to the cold indifference with which he treated his wife. Under instructions, Mabel kept a diary with most of the important anniversary dates for Clark's family. These included his wedding anniversary, his wife's birthday, his children's birthdays and other occasions that required some acknowledgement. Prompted by this diary, she would buy cards, flowers and presents and send them to Clark's wife and other family members at the requisite times. She had long ago given up asking for a signature or kind comment on the birthday or anniversary cards. He was always far too busy to bother. She sometime imagined Clark getting home late in the evening and being greeted by his wife with, 'Thank you, Rupert, for your card and flowers,' which would probably elicit a response along the lines of 'What flowers?' Mabel dialled Smee's number and was soon talking to him.

'Robert, how are things? Mr Clark wants to talk to you. I can put you through to him now. Is that OK?'

'Oh yes Mabel, Please do. I'm just about to leave Belfast airport for Aranmore. Yes, put me through.'

Mabel redirected the call to her boss's office phone.

'Smee, where are you?'

'Belfast airport. I'm just about to leave in a hire car.'

'Good, good. Now when you get to the Keystones' house on Aranmore you are to contact Jimmy Murphy who lives directly opposite and has the keys to the house. He will show you where the paintings are and will help you pack them up for transport. Have you received the photos of the paintings? I sent them just a few minutes ago.'

'Yes. I have both photos on my phone.'

'Good. Once you have the paintings, go down to the harbour where a boat will be waiting to take them down to Tralee. I have made arrangements with the harbourmaster. Her name is Linda Carpenter and she will direct you to the boat. Once you have seen the paintings safely on their way, drive down to Tralee to meet the boat upon arrival. Is all that clear?'

'Yes, of course. All clear.'

'Good. Now keep me up to date with progress regularly.'

'Yes I will, Mr Clark. Goodbye.'

Clark put down the phone and sat back in his chair. He was very pleased. The two paintings were almost his. What had started after a visit by one of his aides to the Keystones' house on Aranmore to discuss the loan was now going to bear lucrative fruit. The aide, an amateur art enthusiast, had told him about one of the pictures in the house, suggesting that it might be worth getting it authenticated by an expert. This had been achieved surreptitiously under cover of a further visit to Aranmore by the aide and a colleague who was a genuine art professional masquerading as an employee of the RPC Bank.

The painting of the young woman was examined closely, without Keystone's knowledge, and yes, it was considered more than likely that it could be very valuable indeed, as it was painted in the style and manner of Sir Joshua Reynolds. Clark had now secured it, and once the painting was in his house in Tralee he would hopefully get it authenticated as an original and sell it for a very large sum of money. With a self-satisfied smirk, he thought how easy it was to make money with all these idiot do-gooders around who insist upon helping others who don't deserve help. What fools they were!

Chapter 3

The satnav in Smee's rented car told him the journey between Belfast International Airport and Burtonport, the ferry terminal for Aranmore on the west coast of Ireland, should take approximately three hours. At Burtonport he would get the ferry to Aranmore and continue on to the Keystones' home. He had never visited Ireland and was looking forward to discovering what it had to offer. He had been an employee of the RPC Bank for seven years and had risen quickly through the ranks to become one of Rupert Clark's trusted aides. He accepted that his boss was perhaps not the most likeable of employers, but the job paid the bills, particularly important when a chap had a wife and three young children and a house in Dartford, a big investment but an easy commute to the RPB headquarters in Canary Wharf. He counted himself a very blessed man that he had a lovely family life. After the demands of working for a hard employer it was a relief to return to the comfort and happiness he experienced at home.

Having made himself comfortable in the car, Smee adjusted the rear-view and wing mirrors and fastened his seat belt. Then, having satisfied himself that all was in order, he pulled out of the airport car park and set off for

Burtonport, guided by the voice from the satnav.

The journey to Burtonport was an easy one. The roads were fairly clear and he only needed to stop once, at a shopping centre in Derry for refreshments. He was pleasantly surprised by the friendliness of the people he met. As it was his first time in Ireland, he was also quite surprised at the large tracts of open countryside and farmland he crossed on the journey, which provided a real contrast to most of the area around his home in Dartford. He was beginning to understand why it was called the Emerald Isle.

He arrived at Burtonport in mid-afternoon and drove straight to the harbour. There were some people about, mainly tourists waiting for the ferry, he guessed. He joined the queue of cars and switched off the engine. Getting out of the car to stretch his legs, he took a short walk to the harbourside and looked out across the sea to Aranmore. It really did look within touching distance and very attractive, surrounded as it was by the glorious indigo-blue Atlantic, itself sparkling like endless strings of diamonds in the June sunshine.

'Good afternoon. Off to Aranmore on holiday are we?'

Smee turned towards the voice. He saw a mature lady dressed in blue, with a nice smile and twinkling eyes.

'Going to Aranmore, though not for a holiday I'm afraid. I'm going there on business. Are you on holiday?'

'Sort of. I've just come back from visiting relatives in England. I live on the island. It's such a lovely place to be.'

'Well, I can certainly see that from here. It does look quite special. How long have you lived there?'

'We moved there ten years ago when my husband

retired. I'm Irish, though my husband's from England. We used to come here on holiday and thought it would be a great place to live. Where are you from?'

'Dartford, near London. I work in London and live in Dartford with my family.'

'I know London. I used to work there many years ago when I was a nurse at St Thomas's Hospital. London can be a lovely place, though not quite as nice as Aranmore.'

'Well, they certainly look very different,' Smee said.

He noticed the lady's car parked next to his as they waited for the ferry. It was a convertible and the hood was down. He'd never been a big fan of cars like that. What was the point, he'd thought, since anyway it was always raining in England. Why go to the expense of getting a car with a detachable roof? It just wasn't worth it!

'I see you drive a convertible. That's unusual here isn't it?'

'It is,' said the lady. 'But you see I've always driven a convertible. I much prefer them to other cars.'

'Oh? Why's that?' he asked. 'Surely there are so few days of sunshine here, or anywhere in Britain, it's hardly worth the bother of owning one.'

'Well, actually I do think it's worth the bother, for precisely the reason you state.'

'How does that work?' he asked, now perplexed.

'It's just because there are so few sunny days, here or anywhere else, that you must be prepared and ready to take advantage of them. I do enjoy driving in sunshine with the hood down, with the wind blowing through my hair – it's lovely. Even if one can only do it just a few times now and again.'

'I *see*. That's sound logic!' Smee had never thought of himself as a 'glass-half-empty' type of person, until now. The lady had just proved to him how the glass could more often be considered half-full.

Smee could now see the ferry boat approaching the harbour, and noticed people returning to their cars in preparation for boarding. He offered his hand to the lady and said, 'Well, must get ready now. Very nice talking to you. I'm Robert, by the way, Robert Smee.'

The lady shook his hand. 'I'm Kathleen, and very nice talking to you. Bye.'

The ferry quickly tied up and was shortly unloading passengers and cars. It was soon able to take the waiting complement of people for the less-than-ten-minute journey over to Aranmore. Smee decided to stay in his car for the crossing, which was uneventful. He sat back and listened to his car radio, and began thinking about his journey and the people he had met so far. He was already warming to the Emerald Isle.

Once the ferry had docked the drive to Jimmy Murphy's house took just a few minutes. Smee parked outside and walked up the path to the front door, which opened before he got there. There in the doorway stood a tall man of friendly appearance who looked straight at Smee and said, 'Hello there! Is it yourself?'

'I'm Robert Smee. You must be Jimmy Murphy.'

'I am that, to be sure.' Murphy grasped and shook the offered hand. 'Come in, come in! We can go over to the Keystones' house after a cup of tea. Sure, you'll be in need of a rest after your journey. How was the crossing?'

'Very quick and no problems at all,' Smee said, sitting

down in a comfortable armchair opposite his host, while a cup of tea and biscuits were presented to him by Murphy's wife, who introduced herself as Anna.

'Thank you very much. This is really very kind of you.'

'Oh, that's all right. How are Mr and Mrs Keystone? It's some months since we last saw them. They are such a lovely couple, so kind.'

'I'm afraid I've never met them. I've come just to remove the two paintings from the house and send them off to Tralee where my boss has a place. I believe the house is to be sold.'

It was immediately obvious that this was a surprise to his two hosts and, from the crestfallen look on their faces, not at all well received.

'Sold? They're moving? But they loved being here!' Anna's voice was urgent and full of entreaty. Smee half-expected her to say, 'Say it isn't so.'

'I believe it has something to do with an outstanding loan owed to my boss's bank.' Smee thought he had better tread carefully from now on. No point in upsetting such a friendly couple with too much information, though he had probably said too much already.

'Well I never,' said Jimmy. 'Such a great couple. We shall miss them. They did so much for charity and always put others before themselves in all they did. A true Christian outlook on life. How much do they owe your boss?'

'I'm not sure, though I believe it's a very large sum.' Smee thought it might be best to get on with his job and avoid any possible unpleasantness with the Murphys, who were both obviously upset at the news.

'Look, thank you for the tea and biscuits, but would it

be possible to go and collect the two paintings? I have to take them to the harbourmaster – she has a boat waiting to take them to Tralee. I can then report back to my boss that all is well.'

'Oh to be sure, to be sure. Just follow me,' Jimmy said.

Smee said goodbye to Anna and followed Jimmy out of his house and across the road to the Keystones'. Their house was large and very spacious with wonderful views of the Atlantic. A very comfortable place indeed, Smee thought. Jimmy obviously knew the house well and went directly to the room where the two paintings hung. As they entered, Smee saw the seascape immediately. It hung facing the entrance door. Looking round, he could not see the other painting until he was well into the room and turned round to face the entrance door. There, next to the door on the left, hung a portrait of a young lady dressed in green. She was looking out of the portrait with just a hint of a smile on her face. Smee stared. He found it impossible to stop looking at her eyes and her face. For those few moments he was transfixed.

'Yes. *The Lady in Green* has that effect on everyone,' Jimmy said. 'But we'll need my stepladder and some ropes to get these two down. You stay here while I go and get the necessary.'

Smee stayed in the room while Jimmy went to fetch his tools. He remained staring at the portrait, finding it quite difficult to tear his eyes away from the image above him.

Eventually, with the two of them working together, the paintings were lowered to the floor and with the aid of bubble wrap and other packaging materials, they were securely bound and protected before being placed in

Smee's car ready to be taken to the harbour.

'There now,' said Murphy. 'All safely packed away. I'll wish you a safe journey, till we meet again.'

'And thank you for all your help – and the tea and biscuits.'

They shook hands and parted.

It took about five minutes to drive to the harbour, and a similar time to locate the harbourmaster's office. Smee parked his car and proceeded to the blue-painted door at the front entrance. Inside, he was confronted by a small desk at which sat a lady with dark hair and dark-rimmed glasses. At the front of the desk stood the nameplate 'Linda Carpenter'. He had the right place and the right lady, he thought.

'Mrs Carpenter. How do you do? I'm Robert Smee. I believe my boss, Mr Clark, has told you of my visit.'

'Indeed he has. Pleased to meet you.' Smee took and held the proffered hand, a small, delicate thing with an attractive ring that sparkled on its third finger.

'I understand you have a boat ready and waiting for me to take some goods to Tralee.'

'Yes I have, Mr Smee. But first just one or two questions. You know – safety regulations and suchlike.'

'Of course. I understand. Fire away.'

'Now, is the cargo of value, and if so is it insured?'

'I understand they are worth a few thousand pounds, that's all. I am unaware of any insurance.'

'And what are they?'

'Just two paintings. My boss wants them taken to his house in Tralee and thought going by sea would be the safest option.'

'Right. May I have a look at them before they are transferred?'

'Of course. Follow me.'

Smee took the paintings out of his car. 'Do you want me to unwrap them?' To his relief, she shook her head, gave them a once-over and, seemingly having satisfied herself that there was no imminent danger of them exploding, she turned and headed back to her office. Smee followed her after locking the paintings in the car boot again.

'Sorry about all this paperwork,' she said, 'but we have to see all the boxes are ticked.'

Smee said he understood.

The paperwork complete, Linda Carpenter led Smee to a boat anchored by the harbour wall next to some steps. He thought the boat looked robust enough for the journey ahead. At first he thought there wasn't anyone on board, but as they went down the steps to the boat, a man appeared on the bridge and beckoned them to come aboard. Clambering over the boat's side, Smee and Carpenter got on board. The man came down from the bridge to greet them.

'Hello and welcome. Balme's my name, James Balme. I'm the bosun.'

'Pleased to meet you,' said Smee. Balme obviously knew Carpenter well. They greeted each other by their first names and exchanged handshakes.

Carpenter told the bosun, 'Yes, Mr Smee is here to help transfer the cargo for shipment to Tralee, as agreed. Is the captain here?'

'Not just at this moment Linda, but he'll be along in a while. But we don't have to wait for him. We can transfer the cargo onto the boat. There's a space for it in the hold.'

'Good idea,' said Smee. 'Let's get that done.'

They collected the paintings from the car and carried them on board. There was a locker below decks big enough to take both paintings. Once they were inside, Balme produced a key and locked them in.

'There we are,' he said. 'They will be safe for the journey in there.'

As they completed their task, they heard movement on deck. Judging by the noise above, there were at least two people up there.

Balme's finger pointed upwards. 'That'll be the captain. Let's go and meet him.'

The three of them climbed the few steps up from below to the deck, and were met by two men, one tall and weather-beaten, fifty-ish, the other younger, shorter, wiry, ginger-haired with large, rough and well-used hands.

The tall man spoke first. 'Hello, hello, I'm the captain. Pat's my name, Pat King. You must be Mr Smee. Pleased to meet you.'

Handshakes all round, though the captain and the ginger-haired man both knew Linda Carpenter well. Indeed, the captain and Linda exchanged a quick peck on the cheek. The ginger-haired man was introduced to Smee as Russell Reed, the engineer, and unsurprisingly, also by his nickname, 'Rusty'.

Smee told Pat that the two paintings were on board and asked when they were due to set sail for Tralee.

'Within the hour. Just as soon as the rest of the crew are here,' was the response.

'Good. And I will meet you in Tralee harbour late tomorrow evening.'

'Of course, though that will be weather permitting. A storm is forecast for tomorrow and we may have to take shelter. But we will keep you informed of our progress by phone, never fear.'

Pat King's manner seemed so relaxed and friendly that Smee thought it must be really nice to serve on board. 'OK. I'll say farewell and bon voyage, till we meet in Tralee.'

'Thank you, thank you. See you soon,' was the reaction from the crew, as both Smee and Carpenter climbed the quayside steps away from the boat. As they both reached a position on the harbourside above the quayside, where they had a good view of proceedings, two other men could be seen approaching the boat, one a young chap, no more than seventeen or eighteen, the other a much older man of around forty. They would be the two crewmen Pat King was waiting for. They both boarded the boat and almost immediately it made ready to leave.

King waved at Smee and Carpenter from the wheelhouse as the chug-chug-chug of the engine took them away from the harbour and the boat headed out to the open sea.

The paintings were on their way to Tralee. Smee could now let his boss know that the first part of his task had been completed. A thought struck him. 'Wait a minute, I didn't see the name of the boat. What is it?'

Linda smiled. 'The name? Why, that boat is called *An Luchog*.'

Smee said goodbye to Linda Carpenter outside her office and thanked her for her help. She wished him a safe journey to Tralee and returned to her office. He looked about him at Aranmore harbour as *An Luchog* continued on its way into the distance. Aranmore was a picturesque and delightful island. What a lovely place to bring his wife Rosemary and their family for a holiday, he thought.

Smee sat in his car waiting for the ferry, which he could see in the near distance only about two or three minutes away. Time to contact the boss, he thought, reaching for his phone and sending an email to Clark to let him know the progress of his journey and of the paintings.

When the ferry arrived, it was not very full and unloading was completed quickly. He was soon on board with a very few other cars and passengers. The passage to Burtonport was soon over and Smee was swiftly on his way along the road towards his next planned stop, two hours away in Sligo town. He was concentrating so hard on the road ahead that he failed to notice the sleek, blue car with two men inside following him from Burtonport, keeping a respectable distance behind.

Chapter 4

An Luchog was not a fast boat. In good conditions she could maintain twelve knots, which, if there were no stops on the way, meant that to get to Tralee would take around thirty hours. Indeed, this was the time given by captain Pat King to Clark's agent when he was hired to take the cargo of two pictures to Tralee. King was, however, somewhat casual when it came to deadlines. He expected there'd be at least one stopover along the way, and more than likely there'd be two. Sure, he thought, they wouldn't mind if *An Luchog* was just a few hours late, would they?

The boat was making good headway from Burtonport, and was maintaining those twelve knots through constant attention to its engine by Rusty Reed. He knew the engine very well, having served with Pat King for the past four years. It was past its prime, prone to break down at inopportune moments, and whenever it did break down, according to the captain and rest of the crew it was, of course, Reed's fault.

Serving on *An Luchog* with Pat King as captain had its ups and downs and was never short of incident. In spite of that, he enjoyed his spells on board and was looking forward to having some time in Tralee when this trip was over. He had relatives there and relished spending time with them.

An Luchog maintained its steady pace and kept chugging merrily away through the mild Atlantic swell. It was now a good four hours since leaving Aranmore and they had made about forty miles of their journey. All seemed to be going according to plan. Pat King was pleased. He had managed to get this job of transporting two paintings to Tralee mainly because of his friendship with Linda Carpenter, whom he had known for a good few years. The fee he was charging for this little excursion was large, over €2,000, which would leave him with a tidy sum once the crew had been paid. The thing uppermost in King's mind was where to tie up for the night. It was now 7pm and at this time of year it would be dark in a few hours, by around 10.30–11pm. He did not want to be sailing in the dark, which he thought too dangerous. Best to be tied up somewhere safe and continue the journey early in the morning. He had his mind on staying the night in Belmullet town. He estimated that it would take, at most, another four hours to get there, so they should be there by eleven. He called out to the bosun, Balme, who was on deck attending to some ropes that needed securing.

'Hey, Barmy, come here a minute. I need your help.'

Balme looked up from his work. What now? he thought. He put down the ropes and walked to the wheelhouse, where the captain stood at the open door.

'Yes Cap'n?'

'Now look. I reckon we could make Belmullet by eleven and tie up for the night. What do you think?'

Balme scratched his head. 'Well, 'tis possible, though

we might be pushing it a bit. I'll go and see Rusty and ask him to try and get a wee bit more out of the engine. And we'll be taking a drink at the Pot when we get there?'

'Of course,' said King. 'But only a little one. We have to be away early tomorrow.'

'Of course,' the bosun said over his shoulder as he hurried down to the engine room. The Pot was a great place for an evening's entertainment, though he was not sure about getting up early after a night there. After all, the pub's full name was the Lobster Pot, so called because, like its namesake, once you were inside it was well-nigh impossible to get out.

When Balme reached the engine room he found Rusty, together with Kazi and William, deep in discussion about the ways of running the old clapped-out engine. William was new to *An Luchog*, having joined the crew straight from school and before, he hoped, going to university. Kazi had worked for King for some years after he had emigrated from Poland to Ireland.

'Rusty, can you get more speed from the engine?' Balme had to shout just to be heard above the noise in the engine room.

'We can try,' said Rusty as he began pressing buttons and pulling levers at the same time as instructing William to reach for a specific tap and turn it on. Kazi, meanwhile, carried on with his task of checking and adjusting where necessary the different gauges on the engine. All this to ensure Rusty had as much help as he needed to keep the tired old engine going.

'Why do we need more speed?' the engineer shouted to Balme.

'We're heading for Belmullet and Cap'n wants to get there as soon as we can.'

'Belmullet! Great! We can have a drink in the Pot.' Rusty was obviously pleased and his enthusiasm seemed to transfer itself to the engine, which began making encouraging noises. William, who was new to the boat and had never been to Belmullet, concentrated on opening the tap as far as he could and then sat down to await any further orders.

The demand for a few more knots worked well and *An Luchog* made good headway, managing to reach the harbour side at Belmullet by 10.30pm. After quickly securing the boat for the night, the crew, led by Pat King, made their way the few hundred yards to the Lobster Pot, which, judging by the noise emanating from inside, was having a busy evening.

King led the crew through a side entrance that took them into the heart of the pub. Instantly recognised by the barman, King ordered colcannon all round, together with pints of the local beer for all except William, who declined the offer of alcohol from his captain and elected to drink orange juice instead. The crew were more than happy with their captain and his largesse. Any thoughts of an early start tomorrow were pushed to the backs of their minds as the food, beer and pleasant company took over and filled their evening.

Chapter 5

Smee had reached Sligo town by six and checked into his hotel for the night. He had still not noticed the sleek, blue car with the two men that had followed him all the way from Burtonport. He was focused on getting to his bed for the night and making a call home to his wife and, of course, keeping headquarters up to date with progress. Having had a nice romantic talk with Rosemary, he then sent an email to Clark to let him know that he was now in his hotel and the paintings on the high seas en route to Tralee.

The next morning dawned optimistic and unclouded in Sligo, giving little warning of the travails that were about to engulf Smee, who, having enjoyed his breakfast in the hotel restaurant and checked out, carried his small suitcase to the hotel car park. As he neared his car, his jaw dropped. It had clearly been broken into. The side window had been smashed, leaving glass inside and outside the car, the rear seats had been ripped apart, the boot lid was ajar and the inside of the boot appeared to have been thoroughly searched. Even the spare wheel had been removed from its fixing in the boot. He stood there, trying to suppress a feeling of panic. Why his car, and what had the thieves been looking for? He went back to the hotel reception and told the receptionist what had happened. She immediately phoned the Garda, while Smee contacted the hire car company on his mobile to inform them and request a replacement car. It was not a good start to the day. While waiting for the replacement hire car to arrive, he thought it would be a good idea to contact *An Luchog* and see how close they were to Tralee. He was obviously going to be delayed and may have to rearrange the meeting time with the boat. He punched in Pat King's number and waited for an answer.

In Belmullet it was 9.30 in the morning and the crew of *An Luchog* were all fast asleep in their bunks on board. They'd had a very strenuous night in the Lobster Pot. It'd been quite an achievement to survive the festivities and find their way back to the boat. Even young William was still asleep, and he had avoided any alcohol – mainly because he didn't like it and he was, after all, only seventeen.

Pat King's phone had a rather unusual ringtone. When someone called him, he and all those within earshot were treated to a short rendition of 'The Laughing Policeman', as sung by Charles Penrose. This would often result in either a number of incredulous sideways looks from those whose ears were assaulted by this or, depending on the age of the audience, a singalong from those who knew the tune and thought it worth joining in. Penrose had been laughing for a good ten seconds before King came round and reached out to answer the phone by the side of his bunk. In doing this he only just managed to beat Kazi, who had been asleep in the adjoining bunk and was not best pleased to be woken up by what he thought was a most abominable tune, totally unsuitable as, in this case, an alarm call.

'Yes. Can I help you?' croaked King.

'Oh hello, Mr King. Smee here. How long before you reach Tralee? Only I have had a mishap and may be delayed in reaching you.'

'Ah, no matter, Mr Smee. We will soon be on our way and will let you know our progress.'

'On your way? You mean you've stopped?'

'Yes. To be sure. Just an overnight stay in Belmullet, you know. We could hardly sail through the night.'

'But Mr King, my boss expects you to be in Tralee later today. Will you make it?'

'Now that might be difficult. Who knows, we may have to put in at Doolin for urgent repairs later today.'

'Mr King, the agreement was to deliver the paintings by today. Don't you remember?'

'Ah yes, of course, but you must know things happen at sea that don't happen on land. But be assured we are doing our best.'

'Right. OK. I will have to let my boss know what's happening. He may not be best pleased.'

'Well, we will be under way soon and will keep you informed of our progress. Thank you, Mr Smee.'

It was not a happy Smee who rang off. Pat King seemed far too casual about carrying out his contract on time – and then there was the inexplicable yet highly disturbing break-in to his car. What on earth was he going to say to his boss?

King summoned his bleary-eyed crew on deck and told them to get under way as soon as possible. All of them, with the exception of William, looked the worse for wear. Yet within minutes, *An Luchog* was chugging out of Belmullet on its way south to Tralee. King was the only one who knew there was one more unscheduled stop to make before they reached their destination.

Back in Sligo, the hire car company had just delivered the replacement car to the hotel. Before moving off, Smee reluctantly decided to contact Clark and tell him the latest situation, though he was far from sure how to go about it. This job was beginning to fall apart, it seemed, and knowing his boss, he felt pretty sure he'd be carrying the blame.

As all this was going on, Clark was on a plane from Heathrow to Shannon on the west coast of Ireland. He had decided to visit his home in Tralee as soon as possible and be there when the painting of the lady in green was inspected and valued. He had, of course, not bothered to tell his wife where he was going or to visit his daughter in hospital. His focus was, as ever, on money. As he'd entered the terminal at Heathrow there'd been a call from his wife, letting him know he was now a grandfather to his daughter's newborn son. He'd told Holly he would try to visit them on his return from this very important business meeting in Ireland, hopefully in just a few days' time. As he emerged from arrivals at Shannon, his phone shrilled.

'Hello, Mr Clark.'

'Hello, Smee. What is the situation?'

'Well, there've been some incidents. It's not very good, I'm afraid.'

'Go on.' His voice deeper, and, to the nervous Smee, disapproving.

'I'm still in Sligo. My car was broken into last night in the hotel car park. I can't imagine why. There was nothing in it. But whoever did break in made a terrible mess. I'll still be able to continue the journey though. The hire company have just delivered a replacement car to the hotel.'

Clark knew from Smee's email the previous evening that the paintings were on board ship, but was now uncomfortably aware he was not alone in this game and thought he knew why the hire car had been broken into. He didn't let any of this on to Smee however, and allowed him to continue.

'And I've been in contact with the captain of *An Luchog*, a chap called Pat King. They did not sail through the night and instead stayed in a place called Belmullet for the evening. Evidently the captain thinks it's too unsafe to sail in darkness. So the chances of them reaching Tralee today are not good, I'm afraid.'

'What on earth…? Right, give me this fellow King's number. I'll talk to him myself and tell him to get a move on. This really will not do.'

Smee gave King's phone number to Clark, who noted it down.

'Now you carry on to Tralee and meet me at Pelham House. I will be there in a few hours. I'm just about to leave Shannon airport now.'

'Righty-ho. See you later.'

Clark was quite sure why Smee's car had been broken into. The thieves had been looking for the paintings. He was not the only one who suspected one of the paintings currently on board *An Luchog* might well be worth a fortune. He knew someone else was aware of its existence, and the possibility that it could be an Old Master...someone who might well try to obtain it and, no doubt, had followed Smee from Burtonport in order to steal it. Whoever was trying to get the painting must have thought Smee would just put it in his car boot and take it to a safe place. Clark had put himself one step ahead. That's why he had arranged to get the thing moved by sea. No one interested in stealing the painting would guess that something so valuable would be moved by such an unusual and comparatively slow method. But this was still a worrying development. He had to make sure the painting reached the security of Pelham House in Tralee. Once there all would be well.

Clark soon reached Pelham House. The journey from Shannon was relatively easy, and he made good time. Pelham House was a large detached residence, built in the Georgian style and dating from around 1805. It was an impressive building set in around thirty acres of lovely grounds. Clark had a number of business interests in Ireland and Pelham House was a good place to entertain business clients. He parked his car in the wide driveway outside the main entrance and was met by one of his aides who looked after the security of the house.

'Good day, Mr Clark. I'll just take your cases to your room.'

'Good, and arrange for my lunch as soon as you can. I've hardly eaten anything since leaving London. If you need me I will be in the study. I have a few calls to make.'

'Certainly.' The aide picked up the suitcases and carried them up the stairs to the bedroom.

Clark sat in his study and proceeded to telephone Pat King.

'Hello, hello. King here, and who am I speaking to?' King's unmistakeable Irish burr resonated down the phone into Clark's ear.

'It's Rupert Clark, Mr King. I believe you are transporting a cargo of two paintings to Tralee on my behalf.'

'To be sure we are. Yes, yes. All going well and we should soon be in Tralee.'

'When, exactly, is that likely to be?' was the curt response.

'Barring accidents we should be there by late tomorrow.'

'But it was agreed that you would be there by now. What has gone wrong?'

'Well, we had to stop over last night for safety's sake, and we'll have to put into Doolin for emergency repairs to the engine. It can't be helped. We're doing all we can.'

Clark raised his eyes to the ceiling, his knuckles whitened on the phone in his hand and he spat out, 'That's not good enough, Mr King. I shall travel to Doolin today to meet you and see for myself exactly what is going on with your boat and why it is that you are unable to meet our agreed deadline. Mr King, you are being paid very well for this job. It is not good that you are not keeping your side of our agreement.'

Pat King attempted a reply to this last statement but he was stopped by the continuous buzz that told him his caller had cut him off.

King was in a dilemma. He had good reason to tie up in Doolin for the night and did not want anything to get in the way of doing that. However, if Clark was going to be there he would have to make sure everything looked above board. He did not want to put his fat fee at risk. What could he do?

'Kazi, Kazi, come here a minute,' King called out to the one sailor on board who had actually served in a navy – the Polish navy. Kazimierz Kasperek was a recent immigrant to Ireland, whose appetite for practical and hard work had quickly earned him the respect of his crewmates.

He looked up and walked towards his captain.

'Yes, Captain, can I help you?'

'We have a problem. Soon we will be tying up in Doolin for the birthday party I've told you about, which is all OK. But the owner of the cargo is pushing me to get to Tralee as quick as we can – and says he will catch up with us at Doolin. When he does, I want you to take him under your wing and make sure he understands that we had to put in to Doolin for emergency repairs to the engine. Can you do that?'

'Of course, Captain. Shall we invite him to the birthday party?'

'Now that's a good idea. We might be able to soften him up a bit with a few drinks and a laugh with us and the others at the party. Yes. Let's do that. And let Rusty know what we're up to. He'll need to be able to prove to our customer we had to divert to Doolin because we had a problem with the engine. We couldn't risk sailing on without getting that fixed.'

Kazi went below to the engine room to let Rusty know what was going on. They had a quick chat and a plan was agreed. They would say the engine needed a replacement for the alternator, which had, without warning, begun to play up, working only intermittently. Why, they had only just managed to reach Doolin as it was!

An Luchog was now about twenty minutes from Doolin

harbour and the captain and crew had just got together to share a cup of tea before they reached the harbourside. Conversation was animated. All of the crew were looking forward to the birthday party that Captain King had promised them would be the party to end all parties. The conversation ranged back and forth among the crew, covering subjects as diverse as sport, religion, what kind of a party they were heading into in Doolin and, of course, politics. At an opportune moment during the political exchange of views, King looked up and said, with a serious look on his face, 'Gentlemen, we can continue this conversation later. Now it's time to tie up. We're about five minutes from Doolin. Come on. All hands to docking stations.'

The crew went to their respective stations and *An Luchog* was soon secure at the harbourside in Doolin. As he left the boat, Kazi took the precaution of taking a spare alternator with him to show Clark, if and when he showed up, as evidence of the emergency repairs necessary to ensure a successful trip to Tralee.

King led the crew from the harbourside on the short walk to Jim O'Malley's pub. The evening was warm and brilliantly lit by the late June sunshine that bathed everything. William was curious about this party. He had only been given the briefest information and wanted to know the full facts. He walked up beside Pat King and asked, 'Whose birthday is it today, Cap'n?'

'William, it's a famous man and a special birthday. To be sure it's Patrick Lewington. Have you no heard of him?'

William said he hadn't, but was anxious to know more. 'And why is it a special birthday?'

'Because today he's a hundred years old,' said King.

'I would hope the whole of County Clare would turn out to celebrate this great man.'

A hundred years. Of age. Old. Ancient. Eighty-three years older than me! William thought hard and even then couldn't quite grasp this figure. How could anyone reach such a milestone and still be thriving?

'What's he done to make him great?' was all William could think of saying. The question hung in the air for a few seconds as King composed himself to answer. This was the first time ever anyone had asked him about Lewington, and he had time to reflect upon the fact that there was a new generation who would ask such things.

'Now William, I take it you know a little of history from your time at school?'

'Yes. I'm hoping my exam results allow me to go further and study history at university this autumn.'

'Good. Well, this man was on the Normandy beaches on D-Day, the sixth of June 1944, and at Bergen-Belsen concentration camp when it was liberated in 1945. He left the Irish army and joined the British Grenadier Guards in 1941 and fought against the Nazis. He is a very great man. My word! Look at all those people trying to get into O'Malley's.'

William looked up and along the street he could see dozens of people outside the pub. They all seemed to be having a good time. William thought he must meet this man who was celebrating his hundredth birthday. This would be living history and an opportunity he must not miss.

The crew of *An Luchog* approached Jim O'Malley's. It was very crowded outside. King led the crew through the main entrance door and they just managed to squeeze inside but could gain no further entry than a few feet, such was the congestion. One of the barmen, standing on a chair behind the bar, giving him the advantage in this very crowded environment of being eight feet tall, pointed at Pat's group and shouted at them loudly above the noise all around, 'And what would you'ze be having to drink?'

King called back at the top of his voice, 'Four of the black stuff and one lemonade.'

Chapter 6

Rupert Clark was in a foul temper as he left Pelham House and drove towards Doolin. The only thing on his mind was getting hold of the skipper of that boat and giving him a dressing-down. Very few had ever failed to follow his orders to the letter – and they had had reason to regret their error. He wasn't about to let some unpredictable idiot of a captain get away with it either. After all, there was a great deal of money at stake. Clark had never been to Doolin and the route was therefore new to him. He was in such a hurry to reach the boat and make it clear he would brook no delay that he even turned down a stop in Limerick to have a look around the town that had given its name to a humorous form of poetry. He had set himself to reach Doolin around seven that evening. It would mean an overnight stay there, but he was prepared for that, having packed a small suitcase before leaving Pelham House. He made good time, driving much faster than he normally did and with much aggression, due to his seething anger. Indeed, he was fortunate he was not seen doing so by the Garda. Still nourishing a fine head of fury, he drove into Doolin and headed directly for the harbour.

He parked his car and got out. The early evening sun

was warm and cast a sparkle of light all across the water in the harbour, which was empty except for one small boat that he quickly found was called *The Talisman*. He had obviously got there ahead of *his* boat. He looked around. He had been so preoccupied with his confrontation with that chap King, he hadn't considered having to wait for the boat to arrive.

There was a lot of noise of laughter and merriment coming from just along the road. Some kind of celebration was going on outside what looked like a pub. To give himself something to do, Clark decided to investigate. He walked up towards the festivities and when he reached the edge of the group of people outside what did indeed turn out to be a pub, called Jim O'Malley's, he asked an elderly man dressed in green corduroy what was going on. Clark's English voice clearly marked him out as a stranger.

'It's my uncle's birthday today. And where might you be from?'

Something didn't seem right to Clark. Hang on, he thought. Your uncle? But you look as if you're well into your seventies, so how old is your uncle? No, this man's already had too many! He's confused.

'Your uncle?' he said. 'Is this a special birthday?'

'Special? I'll say it is!' was the response, accompanied by murmured agreements from the surrounding group.

'He's a hundred today and we'll be celebrating all night. Please come on in and meet him for yourself. By the way, I'm John Lewington. Pleased to meet you.' Clark accepted the offer and shook the extended hand, saying, 'Thank you. I'm Rupert Clark. From London. I've just flown over on business.' He'd wandered into something that was quite taking his mind off the purpose of his visit. He had never met anyone a hundred years old before and readily accepted the invitation to meet the centenarian. Together the two entered the very crowded pub and slowly, led by Lewington, they inched their way through the heaving crowd towards a table at the far end of the bar where the object of the celebrations held court, a sharply-dressed man with grey hair, a warm smile and a small pint of ale in front of him on the table.

'Uncle Pat, Uncle Pat,' said John. 'Here's someone all the way from London to meet you.'

'From London, just to see me?' Pat responded with a smile and handshake with Clark. Understandably, Pat Lewington showed his age. His face was deeply lined and his hair was grey. He was slight of build, about five foot seven tall, and yet his voice was clear – if soft. Clark had to concentrate hard to hear every word he said.

'It's a pleasure to see you, sir, and what's your name?'

'Rupert Clark. A pleasure to meet you.' He thought it best not to mention the reason why he was in Doolin. He decided to say he was there on business.

'And what would you be having to drink? It's a long way from London to be sure. The black stuff, is it?'

Clark hesitated. Generosity had never been one of his traits. In fact he took some pride in his reputation for meanness. Yet, somehow, he felt it not quite right to take a drink from a man celebrating his hundredth birthday. And so, for the first time he could remember, his response to the offer of a free drink was negative. Instead he said, 'That is very generous of you, but please let me buy you one. After all, it is your special birthday.'

Pat Lewington's response was positive, so Clark turned to the bar, where, head and shoulders above everyone else, a barman was standing on a chair behind the bar. Clark had never seen anything like it before. The barman was constantly surveying the packed scene and, whenever anyone looked towards him for longer than a few seconds, he would shout and point towards them, demanding to know what they wanted to drink. Clark soon caught his eye, ordered the required drinks, parted with the money, which was passed from hand to hand by the customers until it reached the bar, and soon the drinks and change were returned, again passed from hand to hand until they reached Pat Lewington's table. A toast to Pat was proposed by John and drunk by Clark and the other friends and family surrounding the table.

In the corner of the pub there was a little stage with a four-piece band, fiddle, flute, banjo and bodhrán. The music and singing were exactly in keeping with the atmosphere in the pub and contributed greatly to the jollity of the event. Everyone was wrapped up in the occasion. Everyone seemed to know everyone else, except Clark of course, yet even he quickly slipped into being an integral part of the proceedings as he got to chat to more and more of the people at the party. Everyone was so full of joy, he thought. Everyone was so friendly.

'Did you see much action?' asked Clark. The others round him were suddenly silent, but his natural lack of empathy prevented him from noting they all seemed surprised at his question.

'Oh yes. I was at D-Day in '44 and Belsen when we liberated it in April '45. Still dream and think about that to this day. None who were there at the time can ever forget what they saw.'

Clark looked at him, open-mouthed, his manners temporarily forgotten. This man was the very stuff of legend! Clark had seen films about the Normandy landings – and this man, still with all his marbles, had been through that hell. Impolite or not, he just had to know more.

'D-Day must have been quite an adventure.' Almost before the words were out, he realised what a crass thing it was to say, and now he was aware of the eye-rolling of the locals round the table, but Lewington took no notice of the mutterings going on around him and responded respectfully.

'It certainly was! Many things stick in the memory: the absolute bravery of all those young men, the leadership, the camaraderie.'

Following Pat's last words, a respectful silence had descended on those around him, all the more noticeable because the band had finished playing for a moment and were consuming their respective pints of ale before the next tune. Clark had no idea how to follow that. Fortunately for him, everyone's attention was diverted by the arrival, through a side door, of a birthday cake carried on a tray very slowly and carefully, by two lovely ladies. The cake was very large and had rather a lot of candles, whose brightness was accentuated by the dimming of the lights in the pub. The noise became subdued as the cake was placed on the table in front of Pat. The two ladies began singing 'Happy Birthday', and were quickly joined by everyone else. Pat looked very pleased with all this fuss being made of him, though a bit disconcerted when, at the conclusion of the singing, he was loudly encouraged to blow out all the candles in one breath. He tried and failed. After several attempts, however, he extinguished them all, to loud cheers and many shouts of 'Well done!' Pat looked exhausted. The ladies began cutting the cake into pieces and sharing them with all the people present. Someone told Clark the ladies were Pat's great-granddaughters. It appeared that almost all of his family were present.

Once the cake had been cut up and shared by all, for there seemed an almost inexhaustible supply of slices, the band began playing again and a space was cleared on the floor in order that people could dance. The celebrations were obviously going to go on far into the summer night. Clark had found a seat near the dance floor and he began to relax a little more and take in the atmosphere. This was a completely new experience for him. So much humour, so much joy, so much pride and respect shown to a great man. As he sat there, he was aware of a feeling utterly strange to him. In the face of this old man's courage and experience, and the obvious love felt for him by so many people, he realised the feeling was humility.

'Four of the black stuff and one lemonade it is,' shouted the barman, and the drinks were soon passed over the heads and through the hands of some of the customers in the crowded pub. King and his crew had arrived just in time to share in the birthday cake, which they consumed eagerly. Looking around, King soon saw some people he knew and set off towards them for a banter, dragging William with him. The rest of the crew did likewise with people they knew. All except Rusty, who, not seeing anyone familiar, decided to get near the dance floor by securing a seat next to a pasty-faced individual who seemed to be enjoying the fun-filled atmosphere.

'Hello there, and how do you know old Pat?' he asked the pasty-faced gentleman.

Clark turned to Rusty and said, 'Well, I'm afraid I've only just met him. I'm from London, you see.'

'To be sure your accent gives that away right enough. Have you come all the way just to see Pat?'

'Actually no. I'm here on business. Though I have to admit it's been very nice to come here and learn about Pat Lewington. Obviously a very brave man.'

'Oh yes, to be sure he is that,' responded Rusty. 'And yet, did you know he was ostracised after the war by our government? They saw him as a deserter who helped the enemy. He was put on a blacklist and found it well-nigh impossible to find work anywhere in Ireland.'

'Ostracised and blacklisted? Why?'

'Because he helped the British. Bear in mind it was only about twenty years after Ireland's independence from Britain in 1922. Feelings still ran quite deep among many Irish people, to the extent that on hearing of Hitler's death, the Irish government sent its condolences to the German Embassy in Dublin.'

'That's very sad,' said Clark. 'How did he come to terms with all that?'

'Oh, he's forgiven all those politicians who introduced and maintained the blacklist. That's the kind of man he is. And indeed, the Irish Parliament apologised a few years ago for what happened to all those brave men who had joined the allies and helped defeat Nazism. Far too late for most of them who died before the apology was issued. However, it's all in the past now, thank the Lord.'

'I see.' Clark was feeling a little overwhelmed by his experiences in this small corner of Ireland. And he was being given quite a lesson in Irish history. He looked at Rusty and said, 'Are you related to Pat?'

'No. I'm just an engineer passing through, though I've known about Pat for many a year. He's a real hero to us here.'

The conversation between the two was interrupted by some very enthusiastic people who had joined the others on the dance floor and were flinging themselves around, almost in time with the music. Rusty got up and joined them. Clark watched Rusty dancing and thought he looked so competent at it that he must have been a professional at some time in his life. The whole pub seemed to be alive with laughter, noise, banter, dancing and good spirits. His glass was empty and, quite out of his normal character, he offered to get a drink for Rusty, who signalled his acceptance from the dance floor. Clark got up and slowly made his way to the bar through the packed pub.

'Two of the black stuff please,' he shouted to the barman in order to make himself heard. The drinks arrived in a twinkling, mainly because, he noticed, there were at least twenty three-quarters-full glasses of the black stuff on the shelf behind the bar. They would be topped up when requested by customers. After parting with some money and receiving the change and the two pints, Clark said to the barman, 'A very busy night for you. When do you close?'

'Oh around September,' said the barman, with just a hint of a smile in his eyes.

Clark found that hilarious and it probably had a grain of truth in it. He turned from the bar slowly, and even more slowly made his way back to where Rusty and he had been sitting, carefully holding the two full pint glasses in front of him and calling out 'Excuse me' every few seconds. It was a perilous journey of about twenty feet. Rusty had stopped dancing and was sitting where they had been previously. Clark joined him and handed over the full pint glass.

'Thank you,' said Rusty. 'And I still don't know your name. Mine's Russell, though everyone calls me Rusty.'

'Rupert. Cheers.'

Pat Lewington was enjoying his party. Most of his immediate family were in attendance. Some relatives had come over from North America and some from England, but most were from in and around County Clare. His youngest great-granddaughter, Donna Reed, had organised all of this get-together and he was very grateful to her. So many friends and family to chat with, and even some people whom he had never met before this night. One was William Wolf, who had managed to grab a seat next to Pat, after patiently waiting for an opening, when someone got up to get drinks. He waited for the right moment and, turning to Pat, he said, 'Pleased to meet you, sir. My name's William.'

'Give me your hand, son,' said Pat, grabbing William's right hand and shaking it. 'And what do you do?'

'Oh, I'm on holiday at the moment and working part-time on a boat to earn some money. I'm hoping my school exam results are good enough that I'll be able to study history at university. The results are due out next month.'

'Well done. I hope you get the right results. Education is a fine thing. Always keep an open mind and never give up.'

'Oh, I won't, sir, but please could you tell me a little about your experiences during the war? It must have been a very difficult time for you.'

'Mmmm. Yes, but there were good times as well. I was one of the lucky ones. I survived it all and I'm still here to talk to you. What would you like to know?'

'The beaches, the beaches in Normandy on D-Day. What was it like coming in on those landing craft?'

Pat knew this would be the first question. Indeed it always was. He had long given up being tired of answering the question. He now accepted his role as one of the increasingly very few survivors of that earth-changing day, and always responded to the question with kindliness.

'I have many memories still, but one of the most vivid is of our platoon sergeant, Ted Smart, leading us on to the beach. He had no fear and just leapt into the sea without any hesitation, shouting, "Follow me!" and of course we did. He was a brave leader. We followed him all the way up the beach till we reached some cover where we began firing back at the German positions higher up. This was on Sword Beach. The fighting was intense and we lost many men. Brave men. Many were my friends.'

William listened to Pat in admiration. A keen student of history – it was always his favourite subject at school – he felt extraordinarily fortunate to be here and able to listen to Pat recount just some of his experiences of that time. He only wished he had his smartphone with him so he could record what Pat said.

'How did you cope with all that? I'm sure I'd have given up.'

'Don't underestimate what you'd do in the circumstances. You'd be surprised at what you can deal with under pressure, particularly when surrounded by your fellow soldiers, all fighting for a common cause that you believe is right.'

'But what kept you going? Was it the camaraderie or the purpose?'

'Both, but most of all probably my faith.'

'Your faith?'

'Aye, my Christian faith.'

'But how does having a faith help?'

Pat thought this boy had a lot to learn. Yet he wanted to try to give him some kind of awareness of how important a faith can be. He looked straight at William, put his hand on his shoulder and said, 'Well, my lad. One thing I can tell you without any doubt, from my own experience, there are no atheists in foxholes.'

William was silent. Christian faith was not something that he thought much about at all. His life had been so full of school and learning that faith had taken a back seat in his life until now. He sometimes thought about his mum and dad, who shared a strong faith in Christian values and were regular churchgoers. He certainly shared their values. Indeed, both his mum and dad had set William a good example in that regard. Now he felt he was faced with someone who was certain that having a faith could get you through just about anything. He had been given much to ponder. William's conversation with Pat was interrupted by the arrival of more of Pat's relatives seeking the star guest. William sat back and watched Pat enjoy the hugs, kisses and good wishes of more of his family. He was truly in raptures with all that was going on around him. He had just one more question for Pat, and he waited for the right moment between all the displays of affection Pat was getting from his family, before he said, 'Mr Lewington, is there anything in your long life that you regret?'

Those immediately around Pat fell silent at William's question, waiting for the answer.

Pat looked at William and again he thought, my, this boy knows how to ask questions! He's going to go far in life with an inquisitive mind like that. Pat looked William directly in the eye and, putting his hand on the young man's shoulder, said, 'Well, son. As I look back on my life it is those moments when I went too fast, dared too much, fell too far, and drank too deep, which bring a smile to my lips and an ache to my heart.'

William was speechless. He thought hard. This was fantastic, yes, fantastic! Would he hear the like again? No. Never.

Chapter 7

The celebrations showed no sign of slowing as the summer evening wore on. The whole night seemed to be wrapped in a golden atmosphere of revelry with everyone determined to ensure that Pat Lewington's birthday would be remembered for a very long time. Donna Reed, pleased that the party she'd organised was going so well, decided to go outside and take in some of the evening air. She sat down near the harbourside, a short distance from the pub. She could still hear the voices coming from around the entrance to O'Malley's. It was going to be a long night.

'Good evening. Mind if I join you?'

Donna turned towards the voice and saw a man of fifty-ish, fair-haired and of medium height, with a half-full glass of ale in his hand. She knew immediately from his accent that he was from England.

'Yes, please do. The party's going very well, don't you think?'

'Oh yes, a terrific do and what a man old Pat is. He's terrific. I'm Rupert, Rupert Clark, and I've come over from London.' He held out his hand to Donna, who shook it and said, 'From London? Why that's a long way to come! Do you know my great-granddad?'

'Hardly. I've just met him for the first time today. Obviously a very brave man. And you're his great-granddaughter? You must be so proud of him.'

'Oh yes, of course. Gee-gee is my father's hero of course, and a hero to many others. We always called him Gee-gee from when we were small. All of my memories of him are of a nice Gee-gee who always brought both me and my sister presents and always wanted to have fun with us. We both love him so much. It's been a pleasure just organising this party for him.'

'You organised all this? Well, that must have taken a lot of effort and time. Did you have help from the rest of your family or your husband?'

'From my family, yes. From my husband, no. You see, I'm not married.'

'Oh, I didn't mean to pry. Sorry.'

'That's OK. I'm hoping to become engaged quite soon. I have to choose between two suitors; both of them have asked to marry me.'

The evening sun had by now almost disappeared into the Atlantic. But the air was still very warm and encouraged a pleasant conversation. Soon Donna would have to return to O'Malley's to ensure the continual smooth running of the party, but she felt the urge to relay her thoughts to the man from London before she walked the few yards back to the festivities.

'Well, that must be quite a difficult decision to make, especially if you have feelings for both.'

'Yes, though I've already made up my mind. Would you mind if I told you about them?'

'No, not at all. Please go on.' Clark was intrigued.

'One of the two, David, is a fisherman. He makes his living sailing from here and catching fish in the waters round here and he's home most evenings. He never misses an anniversary or birthday and loves being with his family – he has three sisters. He helped me organise Gee-gee's birthday party and his favourite time is when he is giving me or his family a treat. He loves Doolin and doesn't seem to have much ambition to leave the area.'

'And the other?'

'That's Jonathan. He owns a furniture shop in Limerick. He's been very successful. He's about to open a second shop in Galway and eventually another one in Killarney. He's very driven and determined to make a fortune. He says he wants to be a millionaire before he's thirty-five.'

'How old is he now?'

'Twenty-seven, three years older than me, and about the same age as David. He has one brother and his parents live a few miles outside of town. I usually get to see him once or twice a week. His business interests take up such a lot of his time you see. He often phones me to cancel some date or get-together we've planned because he has meetings or other pressing business engagements. I do understand it's important for him that he keeps his business running smoothly.'

'And you've already, you say, made up your mind which one's going to be the lucky one?'

'Oh, yes. Once I'd thought it all through it was a lot easier than I imagined.'

Clark was sure he knew where the choice would fall. 'Well, almost no contest, I'd think. When someone's determined to be a millionaire before they're thirty-five, and already on his way, it'd be difficult for anyone to turn him down.'

'Do you think so? Because I've actually decided to say, "Yes" to David and will let Jonathan know my decision next time I see him.'

Clark's eyes opened wide. His hand found his chin. He couldn't see any sense in what Donna was saying. How could anyone turn down the opportunity to marry a successful and committed businessman and miss the chance to become very rich? It just did not make sense to him at all. Were it his daughter, he'd hope she'd have the sense to secure her future.

Even in the fading summer light the other could see his disbelief. 'I can see you're surprised,' she said. 'Let me explain why I've decided to marry David.'

'It may seem selfish to you, but I want my husband to put his family first – above everything – and that, of course, includes putting me first. I want to raise a family where the children know their father and mother and see them every day. Where they can see how much their father and mother love each other. You see, with Jonathan as a husband, family life would come second to business. There'd always be a business meeting to come before a family occasion, before an anniversary, before a birthday, as, indeed, there is already. Jonathan isn't here this evening because he has what he says is "urgent business" in Killarney. If we got married, he'd still always be away on business. His ambition to become a millionaire would be top of his agenda. I wouldn't be happy with that.'

Clark looked slightly away from Donna towards the sea and said, 'But surely you might cooperate with him until he's achieved his ambition? Then he may settle down and spend more time with family.'

The young woman's tone changed to irritability. 'May? Oh no. I can't be dealing with *may*. There's too much at stake. Besides, I'm no businesswoman.' She went on, 'And anyway, most of you men just do not understand what makes women tick. We like attention. It shows we're loved. It shows that our men are thinking of us and putting us first. It's very important.'

Clark was beginning to wish he hadn't let Donna explain her situation. He'd always held to the idea that relationships were second best to getting on in life, in his case, making money, but this earnest and articulate young woman was making him think, and uncomfortably so, about his own relationship with his wife and family.

Before he could come up with a reply, a handsome young man approached them and said, 'Donna, my love, please can you come back to the party. They are about to make an announcement.'

Donna gave the young man a kiss and introduced him. 'Rupert, this is David.'

The two men shook hands and exchanged greetings. Donna and David then said, 'Goodbye,' and turned to go back towards O'Malley's. After a few steps Donna stopped, turned round towards Clark and said, 'A woman is like an expensive Havana cigar. Smoke away at it and it stays alight, glowing. Stop smoking it and leave it alone in an ashtray, and it goes out.'

He had no answer to this. He just nodded and smiled.

Back inside O'Malley's, people were gathering to be close to Pat Lewington's table. There was an air of expectancy, increased when the band stopped playing and John Lewington asked for silence while he read from what appeared to be a birthday card. Donna and David arrived back just in time to hear John speak.

'Friends and relatives, welcome and thank you for coming to celebrate Pat's birthday. I'm not going to keep you from the craic for very long, but we, the family, feel that this particular communication to Pat should be read out at this time. Most of you have known Pat all your lives and know what a hero he is. We all know of his bravery fighting for our freedom in those far-off dark days of the war. Well, I have here a birthday card that pays tribute to Pat and I'll read it to you all now.

Dear Patrick,
I was pleased to learn that you will be celebrating your 100th Birthday on 21st June 2017. I send my congratulations and best wishes to you on this special occasion.
Signed,
Elizabeth R

The stunned silence that greeted the reading lasted but a second or two. Then the roof came off! Everyone cheered and a queue quickly formed of people who wished just to look at Pat's unique card. The band played 'For He's A Jolly Good Fellow' and Donna was not alone in shedding a tear.

Clark had arrived back just in time to hear the cheering, though he was unaware of the cause. He collared Rusty and asked him what all the commotion was about.

'Of all that's holy, yer man has had a message from the Queen, the Queen of England no less. It's unheard of.'

Indeed it was, thought Clark. He knew that the Queen usually sent cards celebrating hundredth birthdays only to people in countries that were members of the Commonwealth. For Her Majesty to send a card to Pat showed the very high regard in which he must be held.

'Thoroughly deserved,' was all he could think to say.

The celebrations continued into the warm summer night, though more and more people seemed to be leaving as the small hours grew larger. The early morning light was just beginning to break through when Rusty said to Clark, 'Well, thank you for your company tonight, but I have to go now. The captain is calling us back to the boat. We have to leave soon.'

'Boat. What boat?'

'It's called *An Luchog*,' said Rusty. 'We are sailing for Tralee as soon as we can.'

Clark's mind was immediately wrenched from the bonhomie and celebrations of the last eight hours back to its more usual state of controlled aggression. Rusty saw a very different-looking man in front of him, eyes narrowed, jaw thrust forward.

'*An Luchog*? Where's your captain?'

'Our captain, that's Pat King. He's just over there, dancing with that woman. He's the man with the beard and green jacket.'

Politeness thrown to the winds, Clark strode over to King, identified himself and loudly insisted he leave the dance floor and explain himself. King was surprised at first, but after apologising to his dance partner, he and his customer took chairs at the side of the dance floor. Clark adopted the aggressive, hectoring tone and the forward-thrust head used when dealing with those he saw as weak or failing to follow his direction when negotiating on business.

'Right. What do you call this? I'm paying you to deliver a cargo to Tralee yesterday and you seem to think you can just stop wherever you like and join in any old celebration instead of keeping to our agreement. I reckon this constitutes dishonesty – and my lawyers will agree with me.'

'Now just a minute,' said King. 'We had to put in to Doolin for emergency repairs. The alternator was playing up and we had to get it replaced. It has taken some time to get a replacement and make my boat safe again. I'll prove it to you.' He looked towards Kazi, who was sitting across from them, and said, 'Kazi over here a minute.'

Kazi joined King and Clark and, after prompting from King, produced the alternator that he had kept in his jacket pocket for just this situation.

'There you are. Just as I said. And we have to wait for O'Sullivan's chandlery to open before we can replace it. Then we will sail for Tralee as soon as possible.'

Clark treated King's words with cold indifference. He was sure he was being lied to. For a moment or two he considered whether he could just remove the paintings from the boat and leave King and his crew to their own devices. He looked at King and Kazi and said, 'That's as may be, but our contract specified for you to be in Tralee by, at the latest, yesterday. You have not kept your side of our agreement and I am entitled to demand my money back, which I think I will do. You have breached our contract.

Accordingly I shall expect what I paid you to be returned.'

'Oh to be sure, you'll not be wanting to do that,' said King.

'And why not?'

'Because you're an honourable man. We have had genuine problems and have done all we can to put them right. 'Tis as plain as the nose on your face you wouldn't do anything to blemish your reputation, would you now?'

Clark was frustrated. Here he was in a foreign country, with likely a different legal system to the one he was so familiar with and able to exploit – and with the odds stacked in favour of the locals. It might not be plain sailing just to repossess the paintings, and as for getting his payment back, his threat to do so clearly carried no weight with these people. Perhaps it would be best to let the boat finish its journey to Tralee, but how could he be sure its valuable cargo would get there in one piece? An idea came to him.

'OK. Sail as soon as you can, but you keep the money only if I come with you on this final leg of the journey to Tralee.'

King thought, and thought. Why not? Yes. Let him come with them so they could be sure of keeping the money. It would be for just a few hours' sailing to Tralee. Should be no problem. He decided to go with Clark's idea.

'Of course, sir. You can be my guest on board *An Luchog*. I think you may enjoy it.'

Chapter 8

Smee had arrived in Tralee and reached Pelham House just two hours after Clark had left for Doolin. He felt weary after the long journey and in need of something to eat. The security man greeted him and showed him to a room he could use for the duration of his stay. With Clark away, Smee could at least relax a little. The 200-mile drive from Sligo had been very tiring and he needed some rest. He decided to get to bed as early as he could in preparation for what might well be an exhausting following day.

Around 7pm Smee was just finishing his dinner. He heard the doorbell chime, the front door open and the butler greeting a visitor. A few minutes afterwards, the butler, Richards, came into the dining room and said, 'Sir, there is a man at the door, by the name of Mr Brittain. He says he's a business acquaintance of Mr Clark's and asks if he might see you to discuss an important issue. Shall I bring him in, sir?'

'Well, yes, all right. I'll try and help him if I can. Show him into the library. I'll join him there in five minutes. Give him a cup of tea.'

Richards turned and left the dining room, leaving Smee to ponder who on earth this was and what the important issue might be. He had little direct knowledge of his boss's business affairs, but thought it best in the circumstances to try to help where he could. If the problem was very difficult he could always contact Clark for guidance.

The library was quite a grand affair, a large rectangular room with comfortable chairs and, of course, many hundreds of books. Smee entered the room and saw a sandy-haired individual standing by the fireplace, dressed immaculately in a suit and tie. Smee approached him and, shaking hands, introduced himself.

'How do you do? I'm Robert Smee. I'm one of Mr Clark's aides.'

'Peter Brittain. Pleased to meet you. So glad you could meet me.'

'Not at all. My pleasure. Mr Clark is away on business at the moment. I hope I may be able to help you. What's the problem?'

'It's all to do with a large sum of money that my company, WTB Holdings Ltd, along with the RPC Bank, have jointly invested on the New York stock market. The stock price has risen recently and we're hoping that we can make a quick joint decision to sell the stock. Your head office in London told me that Mr Clark would be here. That is why I have come over to try and move this forward. Anything you could do to assist would be much appreciated.'

Smee felt there was something odd about all this. Surely it wasn't usual for someone to come chasing a business partner across the sea to get a decision, when there were so many other, much quicker, ways to communicate. Putting his suspicions to one side, however, he thought the least he could do was to try to contact Clark to see what he would say.

'I'll give the boss a ring and see what can be done. Just give me a few minutes while I contact him.'

Smee left the library and went to the dining room, where he rang Clark's number and waited for a response. There was none except an invitation to leave a message. Smee left one and returned to the library to let Brittain know what had happened. It was now 8.30pm. He told him he'd try to contact the boss again in the morning.

Brittain nodded. 'Best see what happens in the morning then. Thank you for trying.'

'No problem. Glad to be of assistance. Perhaps you could call round in the morning and we can see what the situation is then.'

'Certainly. Will do. Are you expecting Mr Clark back here tomorrow?'

'Really can't say. I believe he's in Doolin at the moment and may be there for some time. I've just come from Aranmore, rather a long journey, and will have to wait for the boss before I know what's next on the agenda.'

'From Aranmore? Goodness me, that *is* a long way! Must have been quite important whatever your business was there, and for the boss to come all this way as well.'

'Yes. Rather important. Where are you staying in Tralee?'

'Oh, in the Golden Fleece Hotel. About two miles from here. Well, I'll be off and see you tomorrow.'

Smee accompanied Brittain to the front door and wished him goodnight. He would be glad to get to bed. It had been an exhausting day.

*

The next morning dawned bright, with blue skies over Pelham House. Smee woke late and hurriedly dressed for breakfast. He had just left his room when an agitated Richards came running up the stairs to tell him that there had been a break-in during the night and the library had been vandalised.

'Didn't the alarm go off?' Smee thought surely the thieves hadn't managed to circumvent the highly sophisticated alarm system.

'Can't understand it, sir. They must have found some way around it.'

Smee told the butler to show him the library. 'Show me what's happened.'

Richards led the way downstairs to the library, where they were confronted by the gaps left by the removal of seven of the eight pictures from the walls. The eighth had been severely damaged in an attempt to remove it from the wall, which had proved impossible mainly because behind it was a wall safe and the painting had been mounted on a full-length hinge, making it extremely difficult to remove from its setting. It appeared that no attempt had been made to open the safe. The other seven paintings had evidently been taken away by the thieves. Smee stood speechless for a few seconds, then told Richards to phone for the police.

The Garda arrived within twenty minutes and proceeded to quiz both Smee and Richards on what was missing and what damage had been done. Richards was able to provide a list of the stolen paintings, none of which, it appeared, was worth much. Smee decided it was time to let the boss know what was going on. His call to Clark was answered almost immediately.

'Good morning, sir. Unfortunately I have some bad news, I'm afraid.'

'What is it?'

'Thieves broke into the library last night and have taken all the paintings except the one used to hide the safe. That one they couldn't remove because it was fixed too securely to the wall. I have informed the police and they are investigating as we speak. There are uniformed officers on the premises at this moment.'

'Took the paintings, you say? But they aren't worth much at all!' In spite of what he was saying to Smee he knew what those thieves were looking for. This must be the same group that had ransacked Smee's car in Sligo. They were after the painting that was currently on board *An Luchog*, in a locker no more than five paces from where he was standing on board, watching Doolin harbour slowly receding as the boat continued its journey towards Tralee.

'Did they open the safe?'

'No, sir. They appear to have left that alone, surprisingly. The paintings were all they were interested in.'

'Right. Now keep me up to speed with events and you contact headquarters in London and tell them to send over a couple of security men to Pelham House. I want security stepped up for when I arrive with the paintings from Aranmore. We should be in Tralee by early evening today.'

'We?' Smee was intrigued.

'Yes, we. I have decided to join the boat for this last part of the journey. I will let you know when we are near.

Arrange to have the car ready to meet me as soon as we arrive at the harbour.'

'Yes, sir. Oh, just one more thing. Did you get the message I sent yesterday evening? A Mr Brittain of WTB Holdings was here. He wanted to discuss with you the selling of some joint stock holdings. I told him I would let you know the situation. Is there any message I can give to him?'

Clark racked his brain trying to remember who this Brittain might be, but nothing was forthcoming.

'No, not yet. If he contacts you again, tell him I am investigating the situation.'

'Yes, sir. Is there anything else?'

'No. I will be in touch.'

Smee put his phone away and returned to the library to see if the police had made any progress in their investigation. It was evident they had been busy. One white-coated chap was dusting around for fingerprints while another was photographing from different angles the mayhem caused by the thieves. Richards was helping them where he could. Smee, Richards, the kitchen staff and other staff members had their fingerprints taken in order to eliminate them from enquiries. Smee was relieved that this police operation was so thorough. Clark would have nothing to complain about.

The senior Garda officer, Detective Sergeant Wilson, took Smee and Richards aside and said, 'It looks increasingly as though the thieves knew how to switch off the alarm system. Can you show me where the alarm controls are located?'

'Follow me,' said Richards and led both Wilson and

Smee into a corner of the library where he opened a cupboard door exposing the alarm controls.

'There they are, always left on and checked once a week by me with the help of the staff.'

Wilson was already on his knees inspecting the mechanism even while Richards was speaking.

'Well, would you look at that? They're switched off!'

Smee turned to the butler. 'What! Switched off! Richards, how can this be?'

'I really don't know, sir. We check them regularly, as I said, and there is only myself and one other member of staff who know where they are located. I can't understand this at all.'

Wilson looked from Smee to Richards. 'Who is the other person?'

'That's Proctor, our security man. Shall I fetch him?'

'Yes, please do,' replied Wilson.

Smee did not like the way events were progressing. It would not take an Einstein to come to the conclusion that someone inside Pelham House had switched off the alarm system. In other words, the robbery had been, as they say, an 'inside job'.

Richards came back into the library alongside Proctor, who looked very concerned. He looked at the controls and said to the Garda officer, 'Can't understand it. The system is never switched off except when we test it once a week. It's a mystery.'

'Could one of you have forgotten to switch it on after the last test?' Wilson asked.

Richards shook his head. 'Oh no, we're always very careful about that. We check with each other to make sure all is correct at the end of our test.'

Proctor confirmed his colleague's statement. 'That's right. We always double-check.'

Wilson was silent for a moment and then asked, 'Has anyone else, other than staff and Mr Smee, been in this room recently?'

Smee's suspicions about the visitor yesterday returned sharper than before. 'Of course! Yesterday a Mr Brittain from, he said, WTB holdings in London, was here. He came to see my boss, Rupert Clark, who is away at the moment.'

The policeman showed immediate interest. 'Right. Now did this Mr Brittain say where he might be staying?'

'Yes he did. It was the Golden Fleece Hotel in town. Perhaps you could check if he's still there.'

'That we will certainly do.' Wilson promptly took out his phone and asked for someone at Garda headquarters to phone and check the hotel. In the meantime, the sergeant got a colleague to begin dusting the alarm controls, hopeful of finding some fingerprints.

Smee retreated into his own thoughts. What was going on? He'd worked for Rupert Clark for seven years and had never needed to involve the police before, nor had he ever been directly involved in break-ins and thefts from houses and cars, both of which had happened in the space of a few days. Perhaps it was the two paintings on board that boat that were the real object of the thieves' attention. If that were the case then those two paintings must be worth a great deal. He'd already followed Clark's instructions and phoned RPC headquarters in London requesting two security men be sent to Pelham House. He hoped they'd lose no time in getting here.

Sergeant Wilson's phone trilled and he listened to the caller, ending with a curt, 'OK, thanks.' He put his phone away and turned to Smee and Richards, who looked up at him.

'We have contacted the Golden Fleece Hotel. They have no record of a Mr Brittain staying there. I will need a description of him from you both. Can I assume that he was left alone in the library for a time yesterday?'

'Yes he was, for about five minutes while I fetched Mr Smee,' said Richards. 'And you won't need a description. We can show him on the CCTV images that are taken of every visitor to Pelham House. Come with me.'

Richards led Wilson and Smee to a small room along the corridor from the library. This appeared to be some kind of control centre and at least four television screens each showed different locations around Pelham House including the front door, the rear garden, the driveway approach to the front door and a number of interior locations. Richards knew his way around the room very well and was soon calling up different pictures on one of the screens. All the images showed people, including Smee, entering and leaving the front door of the house. The comings and goings of Wilson and the rest of the Garda over the last twenty-four hours were also displayed. Wilson was impressed. 'Why was this control room put here?'

Richards looked up from the screen. 'Oh, Mr Clark is very security-conscious. He likes to know what's been going on around the house. All this was put in after he bought the house some years ago. You can see how useful it is.'

Richards had located the image of Brittain entering Pelham House and was pointing it out to Wilson while

Smee looked on with great interest. He'd had no idea that this room existed at all and was surprised at the high level of security protection it provided. The image was a good one and showed Brittain full-face.

'There you are, Sergeant Wilson. Mr Brittain entering Pelham House. Do you want me to enlarge the image a little?'

'Yes please.'

As the three men looked at the image of Brittain's face on the screen, Sergeant Wilson sounded amused. 'Well, well. Would you look who it is now? Dearie me. It's him again.'

'Who is it?' Smee asked him. 'Someone you know?'

'Yes. It's someone we know very well indeed. It's Jimmy Wakeford from Sligo. A con artist and thief who's wanted in connection with a number of recent crimes. There is an arrest warrant out for him following a break-in at a house in Cork. He's a dangerous fella, too, and has served at least two terms in prison for armed robbery. I'll put out an immediate further bulletin for his arrest to all Garda stations in the Republic.'

These revelations went a good way to relieving both Clark's employees of any anxiety that their boss could hold them responsible for letting a thief into Pelham House. He had seemed such a plausible fellow. Anyone would have been taken in by him.

As the Garda sergeant left, he told them both, 'Thank you for all this. We'll do our best to catch Wakeford and recover the stolen paintings. I'll keep you up to date with our progress, never fear.' They both watched from a window as he drove off.

'Let's hope they catch the robber soon, and recover the paintings,' Smee said as Wilson's car disappeared from view.

'I'm with you there,' said Richards.

Chapter 9

Hugh Jayce looked at the seven stolen paintings arranged before him on the table. He was not impressed. Although they were good prints in reasonable frames they were not what he was hoping for. He was no art expert, but he knew a little about painting. None of these looked anything like the picture he was seeking to steal. None of them could be passed off as an original work of art, let alone something by an acknowledged master like Reynolds. Moodily, he complained to Jimmy Wakeford.

'Not a single one of these paintings is worth anything. They must have the painting I want hidden elsewhere in the house. Are you sure you got everything?'

Wakeford managed to mask his irritation when answering the question.

'That's all the paintings we could find except the one hiding the wall safe. And that one was fixed with a full top-to-bottom hinge. It couldn't have been worth anything. It was just a front. And we couldn't get it off the wall without waking up the whole house.'

Jayce again looked directly at Wakeford. 'OK. But where is the painting I want? If it's not in Pelham House, where is it? We know it left Aranmore by car, yet when the car was searched, it contained nothing. Not a sign of a painting. Where can it be?'

Wakeford spoke after a few seconds' silence. 'Do you want me to watch the house for any sign of this painting being delivered? Bear in mind that the place is now crawling with the Garda, and almost certainly the security at the house will have been increased. This is becoming a much more dangerous game.'

'Yes, do that. And let me know if anything happens. You know how to contact me. Now these paintings here, I suggest you put them in the cellar for the time being and I'll be on my way. Just one more thing. If the painting is delivered to the house soon, how do you intend to gain entry and steal it, especially if, as you say, security is tightened there?'

'I have a plan that will work. We, that is Jameson and I, will get in without the need to switch off the alarm system. You see, Jameson knows the house very well. He used to work there for the previous owners some years ago. He knows there is a door at the rear of the house that, though locked, is not connected to the alarm system, and he has a key to that door that he kept when he left. Jameson also knows where another safe is in the house. If this painting is eventually delivered, we'll steal it.'

Jayce took some comfort from Wakeford sounding confident that this plan would work.

'Well, you'd better be right.' Jayce turned and headed towards the door, leaving Wakeford to shift the valueless paintings down into the house cellar. Wakeford was a hard-ened criminal who actually got a kick out of breaking the law. Here was no exception, though it was just beginning to dawn on him that this particular adventure was not going to be easy to draw to a satisfactory conclusion. He would normally have given up a projected theft after two failed attempts, but the money on offer from Jayce for a successful outcome was just too tempting to resist.

Leaving the house that Wakeford and his accomplice, Jameson, were using as a base, Jayce got into the car he'd parked outside. Like Wakeford, he felt this operation was slipping away from his control. Two attempts had been made to steal the painting. Both had failed. Each failure would have alerted those who had the painting and would undoubtedly make it more difficult for his hired criminals to get hold of it for him. For a moment or two, he brooded over the possibility of losing the prize, but then he told himself he hadn't become wealthy by giving up. Give it one more try. Wakeford's plan could well work and the information he'd got from bribing Clark's art expert assured him the painting would be worth a fortune. Yes, one more try at stealing it was worthwhile, and if that failed he…no, he wouldn't even consider failure.

Jayce and Clark had known each other for many years. Theirs had been mostly an adversarial relationship that, at times, had bordered on outright war. This enmity had begun when Clark had outmanoeuvred Jayce over a business deal involving some property in London. Clark had made a great deal of money from the deal, while Jayce had not – even though they were supposed to be partners in the venture. Jayce had never forgotten it, nor forgiven Clark, and ever since had been seeking ways to get his own back. Getting hold of the painting of the lady in green would be a wonderful way to get even with Clark. The opportunity to do that had come his way through knowing the art expert hired by Clark who, for a small fee of course, had told him the outcome of viewing the painting immediately after reporting to Clark. At once Jayce had hired some shady individuals, with whom he had previously done business, to steal the painting for himself. He was determined to get his revenge, and that revenge would be sweet!

Meanwhile, at Pelham House, Smee was helping Richards to sort out the library. The mess the thief or thieves had made didn't take very long to put right. The Garda had finished searching for fingerprints and photographing the scene of the crime, and Detective Sergeant Wilson had given them permission to tidy up if they wanted. Outside the weather had turned unexpectedly and decidedly nasty. Black clouds and torrential rain coupled with a very strong wind suggested they should batten down the hatches. He wondered how his boss, on board *An Luchog*, would be coping with these conditions. Still, it was only a few hours before he needed to go down to the harbourside to meet him. He had decided to take one of the security men, Proctor, to make sure the paintings got to the house safely, because he now realised that the two paintings on board *An Luchog* must be very special indeed. When he had first heard that his boss intended to send them by sea to Tralee it had seemed a bit unusual, but with hindsight he could now appreciate the reason for doing it. Clark obviously knew how valuable they were and had evidently expected some kind of attempt to steal the paintings, otherwise why transport them by sea? Smee wondered just how much the paintings were worth. He'd never had any interest in art, but he had to admit that the portrait of the lady in green with the most attention-grabbing look left him wishing he could hang it in his own home in Dartford. But what an experience! First his car broken into, then his boss's house raided and robbed! In all the time he had been employed by the bank nothing this exciting had happened to him. And on top of all that he was in Ireland for the first time in his life, and he loved it. He had already decided to bring his family over for a holiday as soon as possible. He joined Richards and Proctor in the kitchen, where they chatted and drank tea until it was time for them to leave and meet *An Luchog* at the harbourside.

Meanwhile, Jayce had driven to the hotel in Tralee where he would be staying until, he hoped, the painting he coveted was his. He was still not feeling fully confident in Wakeford's ability, following his two failed attempts to steal the painting, but it was too late to replace him. He had to let him try once more before calling time on him. He entered the hotel lobby and walked up to the reception desk, which was staffed by two hotel employees, both engrossed in the screens in front of them. One looked up as he approached the desk.

'Good evening. Can I help you?' she asked. According to her name badge she was called Emerald.

'Yes. I believe you have a room booked for me. My name is Jayce, Hugh Jayce.'

Emerald looked at the screen in front of her and clicked her mouse a few times. After a few seconds she looked up and said, 'Yes, Mr Jayce. We do have a room booked for you. Let me just get your key and the porter will carry your bags to your room.'

She handed the room key to the summoned porter, who also picked up Jayce's luggage. Jayce followed the porter to the lift and up to his room, where he hoped his stay would be short before he could head back to England with the painting he had devoted so much effort to acquiring. The art expert had told him it was almost certainly by Sir Joshua Reynolds and would be worth a fortune on the art market. He needed to get his hands on it before its existence became public knowledge. If news of it got out before he could claim to be the owner, it would be harder to shift it unless he could find someone prepared to buy it knowing it was stolen. That would mean the new owner having to keep it hidden and, of more importance to Jayce, paying much less for it. He settled down to wait, impatient for good news from Wakeford.

At Pelham House, Smee looked at his watch. It was quarter past six. He didn't think the boat would have reached the harbour yet, but he wanted to be there before his boss docked.

'OK. Let's go and meet them,' he said to Proctor.

'Yes, sir. Right away.'

They left by the front entrance and got into Smee's car for the short trip down to the little harbour town of Fenit where boats coming to Tralee would dock. Smee deferred ringing his boss to let him know they would be there, preferring to do that when they had reached the harbour. As they left Pelham House they were unaware of the prying eyes of Wakeford and his accomplice watching for any movements in or out of the house. As Smee's car went towards Fenit harbour, it was again followed, at a discreet distance, by that same sleek blue car with the two thieves inside.

By now the weather was quite atrocious. The driving rain was at times horizontal, the wind was gale force, and the dark sky was occasionally illuminated by streaks of lightning, accompanied within a few seconds or less by claps of thunder. On Smee's car, the wiper blades were sweeping backward and forward at maximum speed and even then he could only see a few feet ahead, and with difficulty. Neither Smee nor Proctor considered the possibility that they were being followed. Their journey to the little port at Fenit, about six miles from Tralee, took about fifteen rain-drenched minutes. They parked a little distance from the quayside, mainly to avoid the enormous waves that were crashing over the quay and drenching the roadside.

Proctor peered through the misted and rain-spattered side window. 'Well, I wouldn't want to be out at sea in this weather.'

Smee nodded in agreement. 'Me neither. This is really terrible! Let's hope they manage to survive and dock here in one piece.'

They stayed in the car, to protect themselves from the torrential rain that seemed as if it would never stop. There was no one outside, except the occasional pedestrian being buffeted by the wind and running towards the lights of a public house at the far end of the harbour a couple of hundred yards from where they'd parked.

Smee looked at his watch for the umpteenth time. Docking in this storm would be impossible.

'Yes, though there's no sign of this storm finishing.

Just look at those waves.' As he spoke, Proctor pointed to a wave that had just crashed over the quayside some 50 yards from where they had parked. It would be a while before this terrific storm eased off.

'Perhaps we could go to the pub while we wait. It would certainly be warmer in there.'

Proctor's suggestion met with approval from Smee, who started the engine and drove the short distance to the brightly lit pub, parking as close as possible. They got out and ran to the front door of the inn, managing to get inside only a little soaked.

The blue car had parked at the opposite end of the harbour, away from Smee and Proctor. Having just watched them enter the pub, its two occupants deliberated on what they should do next.

'Best if we stay here and watch what happens,' said Wakeford.

'Yes, I suppose so,' reluctantly agreed his accomplice, Jameson, who would have much preferred to shelter in the warmth of the pub. Gloomily they resigned themselves to the tedious and uncomfortable wait.

Chapter 10

'All ready?' King called out to the crew as Barmy cast off
the securing ropes from the bollard at Doolin harbour
side. Rupert Clark was in the wheelhouse of *An Luchog*,
standing at King's side watching with interest the crew
preparing for their short voyage to Tralee. He had once
owned a yacht, only a little smaller than this boat, but had
never put to sea with a specific purpose other than to enjoy
himself on holiday or, more usually, to entertain business
clients. This trip was going to be different.

Once they were under way, Clark went down into the
cabin where the crew ate and got Smee on the phone. He
heard the news regarding the stolen paintings, and then
put his phone away and, most unusually for him, fell into
a spell of introspection. This whole business had put him
outside his comfort zone. He'd spent his whole working
life in the pursuit of wealth, pushing everything else,
including his family and marriage, into the background.
He rarely had time for anyone unless they could help him
in a commercial venture or some money-making scheme,
and any respect or deference he showed to others usually
depended entirely upon how much it was worth doing or
how far it would progress his own ends. But now he found

himself having to rethink. Meeting Patrick Lewington and Donna Reed had disturbed him. One had put everything on the line, risking his life and fighting Nazism in defence of freedom and for the good of humanity; the other was rejecting the possibility of abundant wealth for the greater certainty of a happy marriage and home. He certainly thought Patrick was a hero. Indeed, where would the world be today without men like him? But Donna? Surely she could see the importance of wealth. Why give up the opportunity to be rich? A happy home life was one thing, but a large bank balance was surely something better. And yet, was it? In his early childhood he'd been looked after by a governess while his father spent all his time in London working for a bank. His mother, divorced from his father when he was four, had run off with another man and lived in Spain. He'd hardly ever seen her after that. There'd been a series of governesses, then boarding school and university. What was a happy home life?

These thoughts were interrupted by William coming into the cabin.

'It's getting very stormy outside. Hope it doesn't get any worse. We could be in for a rough journey.'

'Let's hope not! Come and sit down for a bit. There's still some tea in the pot if you want some.'

William sat and poured himself a cup. After a short general chat, Clark shifted into career mentor mode.

'Where do you see yourself in five years' time?'

This was not the kind of question that most seventeen-year-olds might have an answer for, but William was more mature than most of his age group and he responded without hesitation.

'I want to teach.'

'A teacher?'

'Yes. Once I've got my degree, I hope to train as a teacher in history or philosophy or both.'

'That's interesting.'

'Yes. I see teaching as being a good way of influencing others in what is right, not just the subject being taught.'

'How do you intend to do that?'

'By setting the best example to my students that I possibly can, both through my methods of teaching and support, and by being involved in the local community through sport or other activities. That way of teaching and acting will, I hope, encourage my students to become responsible, decent citizens.'

'That's impressive in one as young as you. What made you think like this?'

'My family. Mum and Dad always set a brilliant example of service and hard work in whatever they were doing, whether through their jobs or when helping others in the various charities they were involved in – and still are today.'

'What do Mum and Dad do for a living?'

'Mum's a nurse at the local hospital in Cork city, and Dad works as a project manager for an engineering company just outside the city. They're also both involved with local charities in and around Cork. They've always made it clear to my sisters and me that if there's one word that should describe one's life, it's service; service to others, service in the community, serving others in all that you do. I'm very proud of Mum and Dad.'

In spite of the example of his own life, Clark found

himself affected by the dedication to others of this young man and his family. He said, 'I should think so too. They sound like two extraordinary people. You're very fortunate.'

'Yes, I think so. But please tell me, Mr Clark, are you involved in any charitable work? I appreciate that running a bank must take up most of your time, but when you have time to spare, do you help others?'

Clark looked down at his cup of tea. What on earth could he say? His only answer could be no, never! Damn the boy, and damn such maturity. He'd got more than he'd bargained for when he played the coach! He wished he'd never brought the subject up.

William, sensing Clark's awkwardness, broke the protracted silence. 'I'm sorry. I hope this hasn't put you on the spot. I just thought I'd ask you as you were very interested in what I'm doing and hope to do. Sorry.'

'Oh no worries please. I was just thinking about how best to answer. To be honest, I've never really given much thought to charity work. Never really appealed to me.'

For the first time ever, Clark felt a sense of what he recognised as guilt at having to admit, especially to this intense youth – whom he rather admired – that he'd never given any thought to helping others. Guilt! And it wasn't a comfortable sensation at all!

'Well, I expect you're tied up most of the time with running your bank. Must make it difficult to find the time to be charitable.'

To the already long list of the young fellow's abilities, the banker mentally added diplomacy.

By now the storm-driven sea was causing the boat to

yaw and pitch alarmingly, making any further conversation impossible as the crashing waves were now battering *An Luchog*. They decided to join the skipper in the wheelhouse, and they had to fight their way there, hanging on to each other and anything else they could grab as the rain lashed and the wind pounded them. By the time they reached the wheelhouse and tumbled in, they were completely drenched, even though the distance had been no more than a few feet.

'What time do you think we'll get to Tralee?' Clark yelled at the skipper above the now shrieking wind and the smashing sound as the bow ploughed into the next large wave.

'Oh, we should be there by eight or nine tonight. That's assuming the weather doesn't get any worse. This could be building to a really violent storm. In that case we may just have to ride it out. We may well be delayed.'

'Well, I hope not. I've told my man to meet us at the harbourside mid-evening.'

'Have you now? Hope we can make it into the little harbour there safely.' As he spoke there was a spectacular flash of lightning and then, within a few seconds, a tremendous clap of thunder. 'The storm seems to be getting more violent by the minute.'

The three men stayed in the wheelhouse. King braced, legs apart and powerful arms fighting the tendency of the wheel to turn with the thrust of the increasingly large waves that were hammering his boat. None of them said much, preoccupied as they were with the menace of the rising storm. Down below, in the engine room, the engineer and bosun were doing their best to keep the engine going by constant adjustments and corrections to the various controls around the room. Meanwhile Kazi busied himself, at the far end of the engine room, with the ropes and other ship's gear stored there. They all needed care and attention to be maintained in good condition. He was well aware of the need for good equipment, especially during rough weather such as they were now experiencing. He could feel the boat rising and falling in time with the enormous waves, which would produce a sudden crash as the boat seemed to fall through empty space before hitting the sea again. This was not a good time to be at sea, he thought. The sound of the angry depths was interrupted by a loud clang in the engine room that caused Kazi to look up from his work. Worse, the clang was followed by silence. Silence from the engine. It had stopped working.

Reed and Balme rushed around trying to put things right and get the engine restarted, by making more adjustments to the assorted levers and controls of the engine. Above the noise of the storm, Kazi yelled at the others, 'What is it? What's happened? Why no engine?'

Reed yelled back, 'I think it's a fuel blockage. We'll have to take all the fuel lines off and try and clear them. We'll need all hands to help or we will be smashed to pieces in no time! Quick, you grab that line over there and check it for any blockages. Me and Barmy will look at the others. Just watch us and follow what we do.'

In just the few seconds since the engine had stopped, *An Luchog* no longer had any seaway and was being tossed and turned all ways; completely out of control. The communication phone from the wheelhouse to the engine room was ringing continuously, screaming its impatience as King, up in the wheelhouse, desperately tried to find out what was going on. The three men down there were just too busy to answer it.

'They're not answering,' said King. 'Right William. Go down to the engine room and find out what's happened. Ring me back with any information as soon as possible.'

'Yes Cap'n,' said William and turned to the wheelhouse door.

'Just a minute,' Clark shouted to King. 'You can't seriously expect a boy to go out on deck in this weather – it's downright dangerous!'

'Oh that's all right, sir. I'll be OK. And I've got my life vest on.' William pulled a life vest from the pile near the wheel as he said this and slipped it over his head and around his chest, tying the securing ends together. Both King and Clark did the same, though with great difficulty as the boat rolled, yawed and pitched ever more violently as it was now being tossed to and fro by the increasingly huge storm-driven waves. It felt as if they could capsize at any moment.

Clark's fears were not alleviated by William's apparent fortitude. 'You surely can't be serious!' he yelled to King. 'The boy will be lucky not to be swept overboard out there.'

'What do you suggest then?' snapped the skipper. 'We have to know what's going on in the engine room. It feels to me as if the engine has broken down, in which case we'll have to abandon ship and try and reach land in our one little dinghy – which, I have to say, is designed to hold five people, not six.'

Clark was appalled. Abandon ship with a cargo worth millions! No! Not if he could help it!

'I'll go. William, you stay here and help the captain.'

At this point, like an answer to a prayer, the telephone link buzzed. King snatched at the receiver and shouted down it, 'What's wrong? We won't be able to last longer than five minutes more if we don't have the engine working. Can't you fix it?'

At the other end, Rusty Reed shouted, 'We have a fuel blockage, Skipper. We're all working as fast as we can to fix it. If you can send William down to help it will speed things up and even our passenger would be useful if he can get down here. We need all hands to help us clear the fuel lines. Can you send them down?'

'Yes. OK. I'll send them now.'

Clark suddenly realised there was nothing for it but to go out and hope for the best. He and William were out of the wheelhouse on their way to the engine room almost before King had put the intercom down. It was barely ten yards between the wheelhouse and engine room, yet it would be the most dangerous ten yards either of them had ever negotiated. The steep and mountainous seas were terrifying. The two men clung to the makeshift guide ropes that were fixed to the wheelhouse. They clung to each other. They were soaked to the core. They were knocked down to the deck while clinging heroically to the ropes, and after several close shaves with the mighty seas that threatened at any time to engulf both them and the vessel, they made it to the engine room and dived in through the door. Inside Balme, Rusty and Kazi were frantically trying to keep their balance while clearing the fuel lines to the engine. This they were doing by disconnecting the line at both ends and then blowing forcefully down one end. If this failed to produce the desired effect then the line was attached to a small air pump kept in a corner of the engine room, and a short blast of high-pressure air was sent down the fuel line. While they did this they were buffeted by the increasingly unstable conditions caused by the waves smashing against the hull.

Clark shouted at Balme, 'What do you want us to do?'

Balme gestured towards some fuel lines at the far end of the engine. 'Do those next. I'll come and show you what to do.'

As those below tried and tried to clear all the fuel lines, immense waves were smashing *An Luchog* as though it were a toy boat being thrown around by a child in a bath. The situation was extremely dangerous for all on board. Up in the wheelhouse, Pat King knew just how desperate things were becoming. With no engine, he would not be able to keep the boat pointed into the wind. The combination of wind and sea would therefore tend to hit the boat beam on, and in those conditions a capsize would be almost certain. It would take just one wave larger than the rest to do that. What could he do? Landfall was impossible. This was among the worst storms at sea he had ever encountered. He began to despair.

In the engine room the situation was no better. Most of the fuel lines had been checked for blockages, though none had been found. Balme was shouting at the others, entreating them to work faster. Everyone was being pummelled from side to side as each wave spun *An Luchog* around or caused it to roll in the trough between the waves. There was no time to be afraid as each of them tried their hardest to keep their balance, get all the fuel lines clear and the engine started.

In one corner of the engine room was a large mound of old oily rags and other detritus accumulated from numerous past voyages. The rags were mostly used for cleaning different parts of the engine and, once used, were then returned to the pile. No one in the engine room took any notice of this disorganised and smelly lot, as it was out of the way of their activity and of no importance at this frenetic time. Consequently no one noticed the rags moving and the slow appearance from within them of a man of slight build, dressed in seaman's clothes. He emerged fully from the rags and shook himself down. Clark was the first to spot him.

'Who the hell are you?' he shouted. Immediately the others turned to look at this figure who had so mysteriously and suddenly appeared.

Balme, his eyes popping, yelled, 'And what on earth are you doing here? You must have stowed away. Are you mad?'

The man looked at them and said in measured tones, 'Good evening. Michael's my name and yes, I've stowed away on your boat in order to complete a journey. Can I be of any assistance?'

Those in the engine room were staggered by the sudden appearance in their midst of a complete stranger, but also by the fact that the stranger was the only one among them who appeared steady on his feet.

Balme shouted, 'Yes, for pity's sake help us! If we don't get this engine going again, we'll all drown. William will show you what to do.' Balme pointed to William and gestured for Michael to join him. The two immediately got together and to William's astonishment Michael knew exactly what to do.

The situation they were in was now beyond desperate. The boat's sturdy wooden frame was creaking increasingly loudly and seawater was seeping into the engine room. Soon they were all working on a floor that was an inch or so deep in it and seemed to be getting deeper by the minute. Time was running out. Each of them knew that abandoning the boat was now the most likely outcome. It was a terrifying prospect!

Balme stopped what he was doing and turned away. 'We'd better get the life raft out.' He knew it would only hold five, not seven. At this moment the door to the engine room burst open and in came King along with a few more gallons of seawater. He slammed the door behind him and turned to the crew.

He stared as though he were seeing a ghost. 'And who are you?'

Above the roaring of the storm and the pounding of the waves, Balme shouted, 'He's a stowaway, skipper. Must have got on board at Doolin and hid among all the rags. Must be mad.'

'A stowaway? Well, you certainly picked the wrong time and place to do that. We are about to abandon ship. I have radioed the RNLI lifeboat in Fenit and given them our position, though that's something of a guess. They are going to try and help us. There is no way we can save the boat without the engine working. Now, all of you make sure you have your life vests securely tied and prepare to get aboard the life raft.'

They all looked on, mouths agape, as Michael stood stock-still despite the swaying and crashing of the boat and, in clear and unhurried tones, asked, 'Just a moment.

Have all the lines been cleared?'

As he turned away from the silent engine Balme made a gesture of defeat and yelled at the newcomer, 'Yes they have and they're all connected back up. It's made no difference. The boat cannot survive this battering much longer. We have to get off as quickly as possible and try and make landfall. Two of us will have to cling to the life raft's side – it can't hold more than five.' Everyone except Michael looked desperate. This was a life or death moment.

King nodded to Balme and then said, 'Right. The life raft is on the top deck. Follow me now and we'll launch it. Either you two', pointing at Clark and Michael, 'will have to cling to the outside – or is there anybody who'll volunteer to do that?'

'Give me that spanner – quickly,' Michael said to Kazi, who was holding one he had been using to tighten the bolts securing the fuel lines to the engine. He quickly handed it to Michael without a word. The others just looked and wondered what on earth this stowaway hoped to do.

Michael took the spanner and walked calmly towards the main body of the engine while the others watched, transfixed, even as they all struggled to keep their feet amid the tossing and turning. What on earth could he possibly do with that spanner? Michael placed the spanner first against one nut on the top of the engine, then on another near the bottom. The watchers saw no discernible movement of the nuts. Just a gentle squeeze by the spanner. Michael then took the spanner and attached it to a third nut at the front end of the engine, where he left it in place, tightly wrapped around the nut. He stepped back, bowed his head a little and then looked heavenward. The others looked on in disbelief. What was this idiot trying to do?

The engine spluttered into life.

The skipper was the first to react. 'What the blazes!!!' He grabbed Balme. 'Quick, to the wheelhouse,' and dived through the engine room door. Everyone else just stood there for seconds, looks of astonishment etched on their faces.

The four still in the engine room stood looking at Michael, who calmly sat down next to the engine. He seemed to be oblivious to the constant yaw, roll and pitch of the boat.

King and Balme reached the wheelhouse door, only just managing to avoid being tossed overboard by the tempestuous sea. They managed to regain control of the boat, and were able to determine they were just four miles out from Fenit harbour. King began to steer the boat towards safety. Meanwhile Balme called the lifeboat station in Fenit and told them not to come out to meet them as they had now taken back control of *An Luchog* and should be docking within the next thirty minutes. The sea was still exceptionally rough, though now with an engine to drive them forward they could at least work through the waves towards Fenit.

Those left down in the engine room were still trying to figure out how their stowaway, Michael, had done it. How did the engine suddenly come to life? What feat of engineering had been performed to enable such a thing?

Rusty, with a mix of wonder and incredulity, was the first to ask for an explanation.

'What did you do to get the engine to start? Are you an engineer?' Before the rest could add the questions they all, especially Clark, were burning to ask, Michael said calmly, 'I just applied a little knowledge and a great deal of faith. It was nothing really.'

Kazi, scratching his head, exclaimed, 'No, but you must know a hell of a lot about engines! How else could you have brought it back to life? None of us could.'

Michael just shrugged his shoulders. 'Well, yes, I do know a bit about engines, though probably not as much as some of you. And when are we going to make port?'

Rusty responded, 'We can't be far from Fenit. I can feel the sea isn't as rough as it was half an hour ago. We should be there soon, God willing.'

'He's certainly willing,' was Michael's cryptic comment.

An Luchog was now making good, if erratic, progress towards Fenit. The storm was now miraculously abating. The swell remained, but not the mountainous waves they had had to contend with. Those down in the engine room were kept busy bailing out the seawater. Both Michael and Clark joined in, all working together to ensure they reached harbour still afloat. They were all very grateful for surviving thus far and were cheered even more as they saw the lights from Fenit town drawing closer and closer. Eventually King signalled to everyone that they were about to attempt to tie up, and Kazi and Rusty went up on deck to help secure *An Luchog* against the harbour wall. Even within the shelter of the little harbour, and though the sea was no longer pounding the sea wall, this was no easy task for Kazi and Rusty. Eventually the boat was tied securely and everyone on board could breathe more easily with relief at having survived the dreadful experience.

The boat securely moored and the engine off, King addressed the crew.

'Right lads, and you Michael. You'll all please join me for a celebration in the Eastend pub. We're all lucky to be alive after this little adventure and we have to thank Michael for saving our necks. You'll be joining us of course, Mr Clark?'

'I most certainly will,' said Clark.

With that, the seven soaked but saved souls strolled the few hundred yards towards the Eastend pub, the lights of which enticingly beckoned them.

William was determined this time to join in the celebration. He was still some few months off his eighteenth birthday, so not quite old enough to be served alcohol in a pub, but after experiencing such an adventure and close shave he wanted to join in with the others and at least try some of the black stuff. He had never tasted it before and wondered what it would be like.

As the seven men entered the Eastend they were embraced by warmth. At last they could relax and shelter from the incessant rain that had accompanied their journey from Doolin. Quite naturally the pub landlady looked doubtfully at them as they came up to the bar, but she resisted throwing this dirty, unkempt and sodden band of sailors out, especially after King told her what they had just been through and how they had come to look as they did. She was very generous in the circumstances, and insisted that their first drink be on the house. They all thanked her profusely.

Clark felt a tap on his shoulder. Turning in surprise, he saw Smee and Proctor, who had spent the last couple of hours in the pub waiting for the boat to come in. Smee tried, not very well he feared, to disguise his astonishment at his boss's appearance: business suit ruined, hair standing up, unshaven and yet, a first for Smee, a Clark smiling and looking cheerful.

'Ah, Smee, good to see you and old Proctor. How are you both? My, have I a story to tell you! What are you having to drink?'

Chapter 11

The crew of *An Luchog* plus Clark and Michael continued to celebrate their escape long and hard into the night at the Eastend public house. This was understandable, having come so close to a watery end. Their relief at being spared was transferred to others in the Eastend, including Smee and Proctor, who both joined in the merriment. Even William, not in any way used to such high jinks or late nights, became embroiled in the festivities, especially after forcing down his first ever pint of the black stuff, consumption of which, he decided, was not something likely to grow on him! After that first pint, William went back to requesting orange juice when asked the frequently put question, 'And what are you 'avin'?'

As the evening moved into night and then on into the small hours of the following morning, the rain stopped and the wind stilled. Not many of the revellers noticed, being somewhat focused on enjoying themselves as much as possible. Michael, however, was sufficiently sober to announce that he was going outside to get some air. It was at this point that the Eastend's landlady handed the keys for the main entrance to King and told him to lock up when leaving and post the keys through the letter box.

She was going to bed, because she had an early start in the morning. King and everyone else thanked her for her hospitality and he said he would do exactly as she requested.

By now Smee and Clark were together at the bar. Surprisingly, it was Smee who first brought up the subject of the two paintings.

'When shall we transfer the paintings to the car? Perhaps it would be better to do it sooner rather than later.'

Clark waved the question aside. 'Oh, don't worry about them. They're perfectly safe on the boat. No thief would think of them being on board, including whoever has tried to steal them already. We can move them when this party's finished. I'm enjoying this, especially after such a close call during that storm. Coming so near to death, and working with the crew has helped me think a little more about other things in life.'

Smee was cautious in his response. How profound was this change in his boss? Once the immediate effects of the terror had worn off, would it be business as normal? 'I'm not surprised at all. You must have all been pretty scared, what with the engine stopping and the strength of the storm. I'm sure I'd have been frightened to death.'

'Well, yes, at first more anxious than frightened. There was so much to do checking the fuel lines and getting rid of the seawater – the boat was leaking pretty badly – that we didn't have much time to be scared. It wasn't until the captain said we would have to launch the life raft and that two of us would have to cling to the side of it in that sea that I really felt fearful for my life. Up to that point, we'd all been so busy just trying to stay afloat.' There was a silence for several seconds, then Clark mused, 'The whole experience of sailing with *An Luchog* has been something of a revelation to me.'

Smee had never heard his boss talk like this before. They had been together for a good few hours now and Clark had hardly mentioned money, business, the paintings or anything else that might be termed work-related. Mr Clark seemed to have undergone – and Smee excused himself the apparent pun – a sea change in the past couple of days. Would it last?

'And how are your family?' Smee was absolutely staggered! In all the years and the many times he had spoken with his boss, never once had he been asked about his wife and children.

Through his astonishment, Smee managed to blurt out, 'They're doing very well, thank you.' Encouraged, he then proceeded to elaborate, telling Clark how well his wife Rosemary's part-time job at the local infant school was going and how well his three children were doing at their school. He was relieved that Clark appeared to listen with real interest. Smee then seized the chance to ask the same of Clark.

'And how are your family? All well, I hope?'

'Oh yes. My daughter's just given birth to our first grandchild – a boy. I must visit them as soon as I can get back to London. Do you know, I think I really must give more time over to my family. I've been neglecting them. How do you apportion your time with your children and wife? Is it easy?'

'No, it's not, by any means. My job's very important of course, but my family must come first. As I see it, my job pays the bills and gives my family the things they need.

I try and avoid any conflict between family and work, though sometimes it's impossible. I mean, while I'm here in Ireland, my youngest son – he's ten – had his school sports day. I'd have loved to have been there, but obviously I couldn't. Rosemary went though, and she'll tell me all about it later. I try to get home quickly after work and I spend most of my days off and weekends with the children. They have so much more than just the school work. They're doing lots of sport outside school, too.'

The atmosphere in the pub continued to be one of great friendliness and showed no sign of easing off. It was now daylight and the clock that was deliberately positioned over the bar said it was quarter to six. Proctor had joined Smee and Clark and their conversation moved in no particular logical sequence, from families to football, sport in general, the country of Ireland and eventually the question, 'And what statins are you on?'

After a while Clark excused himself and went outside to sample the fresh air and early morning sunshine, which was in sharp contrast to his experience of the weather just a few hours before. Outside, seated on the low wall that ran around the pub separating it from the roadway down to the harbour, he saw Michael, their saviour. Clark walked towards him and sat down next to him.

'Michael, are you all right? Thank you, thank you! I'll never be able to thank you enough for saving us!'

Michael shrugged. He never seemed to show any signs of self-importance over the role he'd played in their survival. 'Oh that's all right. I just managed to hit the right buttons, that's all.' He then proceeded to change the subject by questioning Clark about his future plans.

'And where will you be going next with *An Luchog*? Somewhere further south?'

'Oh no, no. I'm not a crew member. I was a passenger just for the trip from Doolin to Tralee. You see the boat was carrying some cargo for me, and I wanted to make sure it reached Tralee safely. That's why I was on board.'

'Ah yes, I see now. And the cargo. Is it valuable?'

A little of the old, cautious Clark showed itself. 'Well, it might be worth a few pounds if I can find the right buyer. Who knows?'

'What will you do with the money?'

If he were honest, Clark knew he didn't have a ready answer – as he would have had only a day or two earlier. His thoughts had been elsewhere for most of the last twenty-four hours. What would he do with it? If the painting *was* by Reynolds, it might well be worth more than a few million pounds. He could retire and live in luxury. But his financial situation was such that he could do that anyway. What of Keystone and his charity? Could he reasonably, let alone morally, take such a gigantic fortune for himself and see the Ascalon charity collapse? Stop. Stop! What was he thinking? The painting was his, not Keystone's. Why was he thinking like this? What had happened to make him even consider Keystone? Clark's mind was in a turmoil.

Michael interrupted his confusion.

'Will you spend it on your family? Or perhaps you could help some charity or other. There must be some good cause that would benefit from a generous donation.'

Clark was unable to think clearly, which he knew to be unlike the person he had been until quite recently; until he had faced certain death yesterday, and he still struggled to come up with an answer. In some desperation he hurriedly said, 'Oh yes. I'm sure you're right,' and then, by way of getting off the subject, added 'And where will you be going next, after our escape?'

'I have to leave very soon, actually. My boss has asked me to go to Malin Head in County Donegal. There seems to be a problem with a boat there that needs some help. The storm we went through last night is still raging around that part of the coast and it's made sailing conditions very dangerous.'

Clark felt even more confused about who this stranger was. 'But Malin Head is hundreds of miles away! How are you going to get there in time to do anything?'

'I'm sure there's a way. My boss will help get me there in time.'

'Well, how do you know what's going on up there? Do you have a radio link with the lifeboat station or contact with the ship or boat in trouble?'

'Something much better than any radio link. The boss told me where to go and what's happening there. And he'll make sure I get there in time. He knows what's going on.'

'And where is your boss based?'

'Oh everywhere. Everywhere. I must go now. Goodbye.'

At that, Michael got up and began walking along the road away from the Eastend towards Tralee. Clark was going to shout goodbye when Smee's voice caused him to turn round.

'Sir, they're about to serve breakfast inside. We've reserved a seat for you. It looks good.'

Clark got up from the wall and said he would be there

right away. He turned back to where Michael had been walking seconds before and started to call, 'Safe journey,' but only got as far as saying, 'Sa...' before his voice tailed off. There was no sign of Michael anywhere. He had disappeared. Surprised, Clark called out Michael's name, hoping for some response, but none was forthcoming. Where had he gone? The road towards Tralee was fairly straight, so he could not have disappeared around a bend or anything like that. This was yet more of a mystery concerning the chap. He took a few steps along the road in the direction Michael had gone, then stopped. No, there was absolutely no sign of him anywhere. Had he dreamed their whole conversation? He heard Smee again, this time with a hint of impatience in his aide's tone. 'Are you coming for breakfast, before it all goes?'

Clark turned and walked back towards Smee and the pub, more perplexed than ever.

He had to know whether the other had witnessed the same as he. 'Did you see Michael then? I was chatting with him when you first called out. We were sitting together on the wall. Did you see him?'

Smee looked oddly at his boss and said, 'No. Only saw you on the wall when I came out. Come on. The breakfast is lovely, I just hope there's plenty left for you!'

Inside the Eastend, the noisy merriment of the night had been replaced by the clinking sound of knives and forks on plates as the hungry and mostly slightly tipsy crew devoured their breakfast. The landlady and her husband had indeed made an early start by cooking a large breakfast for the crew and serving them at the tables in the bar. Although alcohol was no longer being consumed, it was indeed surprising that no one had fallen asleep. Perhaps hunger had allowed everyone to remain alive to the world. Clark made short work of his breakfast, as did nearly everyone. The landlady's husband collected all the plates and cutlery, during which he was overwhelmed by a constant barrage of 'thank yous' and 'well dones' from the very appreciative guests. Pat King asked Clark where Michael had gone. He replied that he last saw him walking towards Tralee.

'Well, 'tis a shame he didn't stay for breakfast and we could all have thanked him again for saving us. I wonder where he's gone.'

Clark was beginning to suspect that there were no answers that would make any rational sense concerning Michael's appearance and disappearance, something his logical brain found disconcerting. What Michael had said about going to Malin Head may well have prompted some incredulous comments. He decided to keep quiet and his own counsel for the moment.

'Are we ready to transfer the paintings to our car?' Smee asked his boss as they both, with Proctor, sipped at their coffee.

'Yes,' said Clark. 'Just let me settle our bill and we can go down to the boat and get them.'

He got up and approached the landlady, who was resting in a chair by the bar.

'Can we have our bill please? Thank you for a terrific night and a superb breakfast.'

'Thank you, but no need to pay, sir,' was the reply. 'Your bill has been settled by Mr King, though if you would like to leave a tip it would be much appreciated.'

One more surprise for Mr Clark, who said that he would certainly leave a tip. He thanked the landlady again and turned to King, who was sitting sipping coffee with Kazi, Barmy, Rusty and William, all of whom appeared reasonably sober.

'Mr King, this is very generous of you. Thank you indeed. Now may we get my paintings from the boat?'

'Of course. Rusty will accompany you down to the boat to get them. And as this is a parting, may I say, "God bless you and all the best for the future." Our time together will never be forgotten. Not by any of us, I'm sure.'

Clark and his party shook hands with King and the rest of the crew. There was much backslapping and many exchanges of good wishes between everyone. They all had, indeed, shared quite an adventure.

Pat King's parting words to them were, 'If only Michael our saviour had stayed with us to say "goodbye". We all owe him a debt of gratitude. I say we wish him God speed in whatever he is doing and wherever he may be.' Words echoed by all with enthusiasm.

Led by Rusty, Clark's party went along the road towards *An Luchog* with the others' shouts of farewell ringing in their ears. Once on board, Rusty opened the locker containing the paintings and handed them, one each, to Clark and Smee. All four men walked back along the road towards the Eastend, where the car that would take Clark back to his home was parked. Once the paintings were safely stowed in the boot, they all said goodbye to Rusty and got in the car. Proctor drove and, easing the car out on to the road, they set off towards Pelham House.

The short journey from the harbour at Fenit to Tralee

and Clark's house was made mostly in silence. Clark spent most of the time thinking about Michael and their conversation on the wall outside the Eastend. But how had he disappeared so quickly? Was he some kind of magician? He found once again that, unusually for him, he had no answers to these questions. Perhaps he needed to discuss them all with someone. That might help.

None of them in the car noticed the sleek, blue machine that followed them to Tralee and Pelham House. The two occupants of the blue car were both very tired and hungry, having spent the entire night in the car, waiting and watching with nothing to eat. They'd seen the paintings transported between *An Luchog* and Proctor's car, so they now knew exactly where they were. They were getting closer to securing them, they thought.

Clark's party soon reached Pelham House and stopped the car outside the main entrance. Smee and Proctor unloaded the paintings and took them to the library, where they were unpacked and placed on a table against the wall. Clark immediately got on the phone and contacted the art expert he had lined up to come and view the paintings and hopefully begin the process of proving that *The Lady in Green* was by Sir Joshua Reynolds. This expert, for obvious reasons, was not the one he had previously used to view the painting on Aranmore, and had said he would be arriving in the early afternoon that very day.

Smee and Proctor had lunch together. Clark ate alone in his study, and was still lost in thought. The art expert, Henderson, arrived at 2.30pm and was shown into Pelham House by the butler and directed to the library, where Clark and Smee were waiting with the two paintings.

'Good afternoon, and welcome to my home, Mr Henderson,' said Clark. 'I'm Rupert and this is my aide, Robert. And here are the two paintings.' Clark led Henderson towards the table where the two works of art were standing.

'Thank you for asking me here,' said Henderson. 'Please, call me Richard.'

He moved closer to the paintings and gave the seascape a quick look-over.

'Ah, yes. Not by anyone I recognise. A nice painting though.' It was clear from his voice that he did not think that painting had much value. He then switched his attention to the portrait of the lady in green and proceeded to examine it in great detail with the aid of a magnifying glass that he produced from his inside pocket. This intense scrutiny lasted for at least ten minutes while Clark and Smee sat expectantly watching Henderson going about his work. The expert's examination was accompanied by lots of 'ahhs' and 'mmms' before he finally stepped back from the painting, turned round and, looking straight at Clark, said, 'Well, it's certainly a magnificent example of the genre. I have rarely, if ever, seen better. The way she looks out of the painting is eye-catching to say the least. The sitter for this must have been quite a lady and, no doubt, a look from those eyes would have smitten most men. I'm impressed.'

Clark could contain himself no longer.

'Yes, but is it a Reynolds?'

Henderson, looking at the painting, said, 'Well, there are definite signs here that—'

Clark interrupted, 'How could any painting by someone so famous have escaped the art world's attention for so many years? How could something so potentially valuable have lain hidden for so long?'

Henderson thought for a moment. 'Yes it could. I can think of a number of examples by other artists where paintings of note have become lost to the art world, indeed lost to the world in general, and have then turned up unexpectedly. This may be one of those occasions.'

Clark latched on to Henderson's last comment. 'What do you mean? Are you saying that this painting is valuable?'

'Having now seen the painting for myself, having viewed its quality and its tremendously eye-catching sitter, I would say I am ninety per cent certain this is a work by Sir Joshua Reynolds. It's an absolutely stunning portrait. Where did you get it?'

Neither Clark nor Smee could contain themselves any longer. Clark let out a delighted, 'Yeeees!' while Smee confined himself to a gentle whistle of appreciation.

'It's been in a house on the Isle of Aranmore for many years,' said Clark. 'That's probably why no one in the art world knew of its existence. But how much do you think it might be worth?'

Henderson furrowed his brow, looked again at the painting, thought for a few seconds and said, 'Well, the market is pretty hot at the moment and something like this would provoke a lot of interest. I would expect it to realise somewhere between £4 and £5 million. It has certainly got presence. Yes, it will fetch a very good price I think.'

Clark was ecstatic. This would be his greatest coup! All his effort had been worthwhile, but what would or should he do with the money this painting now seemed certain to realise? He was happy and at the same time very thoughtful.

Clark thanked Henderson for his valuation of *The Lady in Green*, and after a celebratory glass of champagne with everyone, Henderson left soon afterwards, by taxi, to catch a flight from Cork back to London. Clark and Smee said goodbye to him from the front door of Pelham House and then went back inside to have dinner. Proctor was called to take the portrait of the lady in green and lock it in the downstairs safe, which was just about big enough to take it.

At some distance from Pelham House, Wakeford, leaning on his car's roof in order to steady his hands while holding a pair of binoculars, saw Henderson's taxi leave. He had made sure the house was under constant surveillance since his conversation with Jayce and he had seen the two paintings taken from the boot of Proctor's car and into the house, as well as Henderson's arrival and departure. He knew the painting his current employer wanted so badly was inside Pelham House. He decided to move quickly to steal it. He would break in to the house that very evening, only this time he would take Jameson with him to help locate the painting as rapidly as possible. He knew what it looked like, having had a detailed description of it from Jayce. And Jameson would be a great help to him, having been a previous employee at the house and knowing its layout, and the location of another safe in the house. What could possibly go wrong with his plan?

Chapter 12

Clark and Smee dined together in Pelham House that evening. Much of their conversation was about *The Lady in Green* and Henderson; however Clark kept returning to the subject uppermost in his mind: *An Luchog* and its crew. Smee adopted the subsidiary role of listening to his boss and occasionally asking questions as the opportunities arose. The whole affair of the last few days had been a revelation to him. His first experience of Ireland; the personalities of the crew of *An Luchog*; his brush with the criminal class; Pelham House, and his boss's admission that perhaps life is not necessarily all about the pursuit of money. What a lot to tell his dear wife when he returned home. Clark eventually got round to talking about Michael and his disappearance. It was clearly causing him wonder – and anxiety. Something he just could not satisfactorily explain, no matter how many times he talked it through with Smee.

'And I still can't work out how he managed to get that engine going,' said Clark. 'If I were a religious man I'd say it could only be a miracle, but I'm not, so there must be a logical explanation. But what?'

Smee asked, 'Did any of the boat's crew come up with

a satisfactory explanation? After all, I'm sure there'd have been some of them who were very familiar with the workings of that engine.'

'No, nothing from any of them. They were all as surprised as I was. We were all preparing to abandon ship and launch the life raft when suddenly, out from a pile of rags comes Michael – a stowaway. Then, just as Captain King finally ordered us to launch the life raft, he quietly proceeds to restart the engine, by what means I just don't know, and almost certainly save us all from a watery grave. Miracles don't happen, so how did he do it?'

This last sentence hung in the air for some time as Clark wrestled with it. Smee just stayed silent to allow that thought to settle in Clark's mind. Smee was a Christian and a firm believer in the possibility of miracles, although he thought it best if he did not get into an argument with his boss about whether or not miracles happen. They eventually finished their discussion and retired for the night, making sure that the alarm system was switched on. Both Proctor and an aide were positioned ready to prevent any attempt to steal *The Lady in Green* during the night.

Wakeford left the house he was renting soon after midnight and drove with Jameson towards Pelham House. They parked about half a mile from their destination and walked to within a few hundred yards of the rear of the building. Jameson led Wakeford to an entrance used by the staff. 'It's not alarmed. At least, it wasn't when I worked at the house.' They clambered over the boundary wall and slowly approached this small entrance on the ground floor of the now dark and quiet Pelham House. The door was locked, of course, though this was not a problem for them. Jameson had a key that he'd kept when he left the employ of the previous owner of Pelham House, some four years previously. Jameson inserted the key into the lock and slowly turned it. It worked. The door opened and they both entered slowly and quietly, shutting the door behind them.

Jameson whispered to Wakeford, 'OK. Now there is a safe on this floor that is quite capable of holding a couple of large paintings. It's along the corridor and through another room. Follow me.'

Wakeford kept very close to Jameson as they made their way along the corridor and into a small room, the only light to aid them coming from the torches they each carried. Once inside the small room, they closed the door and Jameson directed the light from his torch towards another door in the corner of the room.

'That's it. Through there.'

The two shuffled gingerly across the room towards the door and Jameson opened it slowly. It creaked. They went into the room and closed the creaking door behind them. Jameson pointed with his torch towards the far wall. 'There it is, just where it always was.'

The safe was surrounded by cupboards on each side and looked old. Wakeford walked up to it and looked at it closely. 'It's a Milner's safe. Must be a hundred years old at least. This qualifies as an antique in its own right. This won't be a problem to break into. I grew up with these safes.'

Wakeford put down the briefcase he had been carrying next to the safe and, opening it, produced a stethoscope that he then put around his neck and up to his ears. He then presented the business end of the device to the door of the safe, positioned next to the tumbler lock. Jameson watched with interest, holding his torch so Wakeford could adequately see what he was doing. Slowly but surely, Wakeford turned the tumbler lock backward and forward until he detected the correct noise. The entire process took no longer than ten minutes while Jameson looked on with increasing curiosity and admiration. Then Wakeford uttered a satisfied, 'Ahhhhh, that's it,' and grabbed the safe door handle, giving it a sharp anticlockwise turn. The door gave a loud click and opened up to reveal its contents, which the two burglars could see was a single painting.

'Well, well. You made that look very easy.'

The voice was neither Jameson's nor Wakeford's, but Proctor's.

'And stay exactly where you are. The Garda are on their way.'

At the same time the room was suddenly lit up as the main lights were switched on and Proctor emerged from behind the curtains with Jones, his colleague, each holding what appeared to be some kind of cosh.

Wakeford and Jameson were in shock, Jameson only managing to utter, 'What the—' before he was interrupted by the sound of a police siren outside the house. This was quickly followed by the banging of doors and soon the room was full of Garda, accompanied by Clark and Smee in their dressing gowns.

In this situation any resistance by either of the two crooks was futile. They'd been caught red-handed! They were both handcuffed and escorted to the waiting police cars outside the house. Wakeford was the only one to speak. 'How did you know? How did you know we were coming? Did someone grass on us?'

'Save your questions for later,' said Clark.

'Or perhaps you might help yourself by telling us who hired you,' said one of the uniformed Garda officers.

No answer to the last question was forthcoming from Wakeford and he and Jameson were soon on their way to the police cells in Tralee.

The Garda sergeant stayed behind with Clark and Smee, taking details of what had happened and reviewing the CCTV images of the break-in, which, though taken mostly in the dark, still showed enough of the two assailants, thanks to the thermal imaging, to ensure they would be locked up for some time.

It was almost four in the morning before the Garda sergeant left Pelham House, having taken notes and copies of the CCTV pictures as evidence.

'Thank you for your help, sir,' the sergeant said to Clark. 'Rest assured these two will be locked away, and if there was a third party involved, we will catch him. I shall return tomorrow afternoon to interview you further and take more details of what the two were hoping to steal.'

Clark, Smee and the others said goodbye to the police sergeant until the following afternoon. It had been a successful evening.

Far too awake now to try to get back to sleep, Clark ordered an early breakfast, and was joined in the dining room by Smee and Proctor. They ate heartily, discussing the events of the past evening and congratulating themselves on capturing the thieves. Proctor told them he remembered Jameson from the time when he was employed at Pelham House, saying, 'I always felt he was not quite a hundred per cent you know.'

Smee nodded and said nothing, only thinking that hindsight would forever have perfect vision.

Meanwhile Wakeford sat in the interview room at the Garda station in Tralee feeling pretty miserable. The questions being fired at him by the two detectives were largely unanswerable without further incriminating himself and, of course, his paymaster. He knew his defence was a lost cause.

'We know you were not acting on your own initiative with Jameson. Someone was paying you to do this. Who was it?' Wakeford knew the detective who put this question. His name was Wilson. They had met before when Wakeford had been a suspect in another break-in. He said nothing.

'Silence really isn't an option. With your record you'll almost certainly get at least four years for this. Tell us who's behind all this and you may well get a lighter sentence for helping us. Come on man, think about yourself.'

The argument was very persuasive. What could he do? What was the point in protecting his employer? He decided to tell all.

'Jayce is his name, Hugh Jayce. That's all I know. I think he's staying in a hotel nearby. I contact him by telephone.'

'What's his number?' asked Wilson.

Wakeford quoted the number he had been given, from memory. He was not one to write such things down – too incriminating.

Wilson wrote down the number and left the interview room. Wakeford was escorted back to his cell, hoping his cooperation would result in a much shorter sentence. He had been in prison before, in Cork city, and was not looking forward to another spell behind bars.

Wilson took the telephone number directly to the Special Operations Office on the top floor of the building. There he explained the situation to the head of the department, who took him into a large room at the rear of the building that was staffed by a number of people, almost all of whom were busy staring at computer screens. The department head interrupted one of the workers and handed her the telephone number, saying, 'Maolisa. Put this number in and tell me where the phone is please.'

Maolisa entered the phone number into her computer, pressed a few more keys very quickly and in seconds the computer screen was lit with a map of Tralee. All three of them stared hard at the screen. A flashing blue dot secured their attention on the map.

'That's Dan Spring Road, near the centre of Tralee. The Rosebud Hotel. I can't tell you what floor it's on, but that's where the phone is.'

'Thank you, Maolisa. Very good, thank you.' Detective Wilson left the Garda station with two other plain clothes detectives and in an unmarked car headed towards the centre of Tralee, and the Rosebud Hotel.

Hugh Jayce had also been unable to sleep and so was enjoying an early breakfast in the Rosebud Hotel. He wondered how Wakeford was progressing in his attempt to secure the painting. He thought he would give him one more day before pulling the plug on this exercise and getting back to his home in London. He still considered himself fortunate to have found out about the existence of the painting through his contact with the art expert. He didn't intend to do the actual theft himself, but the opportunity to secure something so rare, valuable and, at present, unknown, had been too tempting – especially for one who had spent years dealing in paintings and other visual arts, on the shadier side of the art market. There would also be the pleasure of getting one over on Clark. Jayce still resented the way Clark had outmanoeuvred him on that business deal in the past. If this opportunity failed, no matter. He had plenty of other prospects ongoing and one day he would find a way to punish Clark.

'Good morning. Are you Mr Jayce?'

Jayce looked up from his bacon and eggs. 'Yes, that's me. What do you want?'

'I am Detective Sergeant Wilson and these are my two colleagues. I have a warrant for your arrest concerning the attempted theft of a painting this morning from the home of Rupert Clark in Tralee. We have sworn statements from one of the thieves that he was in your employment. You do not have to say anything. But it may harm your defence if you do not mention when questioned something which you later rely on in court. Anything you do say may be given in evidence.'

Jayce sat open-mouthed and dropped his fork on the plate.

'It's not true. It's a lie! You can't be serious.' The words tumbled from his mouth as he tried to overcome the shock of being arrested.

'I can assure you, sir, that we are deadly serious.

I must ask you to accompany me to the station, where your statement will be taken. You may contact a solicitor there if you wish.'

Wilson stepped back to allow Jayce to get up from the table. The other guests had stopped eating their breakfast in order to observe this surprising occurrence more closely. Most of them had never seen an arrest before, so for them this was a unique occasion and quite entertaining! Jayce was escorted to his room to collect his belongings and then driven, under close guard, to the Garda station.

For Jayce and his criminal associates, Wakeford and Jameson, the attempt to steal *The Lady in Green* had ended in failure.

Chapter 13

At Pelham House it was early in the afternoon and Clark, Smee and Proctor were waiting together in the library for the return of the Garda to take their statements. They did not have long to wait. Wilson arrived with one other policeman who was there to record the statements, and they all sat together while Wilson asked the questions.

The sergeant told them of the arrest of Jayce, the apparent mastermind behind the attempts to steal the painting. This news was greeted with enthusiasm and they all congratulated Wilson and his team. After about an hour the interview finished and the two officers left. Clark and Smee stayed in the library, while Proctor had other business to attend to. It had been a hectic couple of days and both of them were beginning to feel rather tired. They settled in the comfortable chairs in the library and the butler fetched them drinks. Flights were booked for both of them to fly back to London from Cork the following day. Smee was really looking forward to being with his family again after being away these last few days. He had much to tell Rosemary.

'Well, Robert. I think we have both had quite an exceptional experience here in Ireland. I'll certainly never forget the crew of *An Luchog*. What a bunch! And Michael, I still can't work him out.'

Smee was surprised at this degree of familiarity from his boss. He was slightly unsure about how to respond. Sensing this, Clark said, 'Oh, please call me Rupert or even Rupe. We've known each other long enough and we've shared something quite unique. After all, friendship is about shared experiences.'

Smee couldn't help wondering if the whiskey they were sharing had had a transforming effect on his boss's thinking. But no, he thought, he hasn't had enough for that. Maybe he was actually becoming friendlier as a result of his recent experiences. He decided to take him at his word and give it a try.

'Well, Rupert...' Smee almost couldn't go on. It was just so difficult after six years to call his usually distant boss by his Christian name. It reminded him of when he was at school and the new maths teacher insisted upon all the pupils calling him by his Christian name, George, instead of 'sir' or 'Mr Jones' as they were used to addressing their teachers. 'The more you tell me about Michael, the more convinced I am that there's something which can't be explained. Why, at the precise moment you and the crew were in the most danger, would a complete stranger suddenly appear and, by using just a spanner, manage to get the engine firing on all cylinders? I don't think there can be a logical explanation. I mean, Balme and Rusty had worked with the engine for years. They'd have known its every little shortcoming, yet they weren't able to get it to start.'

'You mean that there can only be a supernatural explanation?' mused Clark.

'Well, yes. I think so.'

'Steady on,' said Clark. 'You're getting into alien territory for me. I've never believed in the supernatural – angels, Jesus and all that stuff, or a Supreme Being. Life on earth just happened by accident, didn't it?'

'You mean by complete accident?'

'Yes, of course.'

'I'm not so sure of that. Greater minds than mine, even atheists, have wondered how life began. Take Sir Fred Hoyle, for example—'

Clark interrupted. 'Fred Hoyle the astronomer? What did he say about it?'

Smee continued, 'Well, if my memory is correct, he said something along the lines of, "The chance that life on earth might have emerged by accident is comparable to a tornado sweeping through a junkyard and assembling a Boeing 747 jetliner from the materials therein." If one accepts Hoyle's proposition then it's definitely possible that a Supreme Being, let's call him God for the purposes of argument, designed life on earth. Therefore I'd suggest he could well have designed someone like Michael to come along and save you all at just the right time. Perhaps we could call Michael a guardian angel for want of a better expression.'

Clark's mind was in turmoil. What Smee had just told him about the tornado, the 747 and Fred Hoyle was a thought-provoking revelation to him. He had never considered things in that way. He had always dismissed God from his thoughts, believing firmly in the power of money to the exclusion of all else. But he had to admit to himself that there was no sensible answer to the circumstances around the saving of *An Luchog* and everyone on board. He stayed quiet and poured each of them another whiskey.

As the evening wore on and the whiskey flowed increasingly freely, Clark became more animated in expressing his views and thoughts, and the conversation between the two of them became more like a chat between old friends rather than between master and servant. The library at Pelham House had become, for that evening, a place of discussion about almost every subject imaginable. To Smee's surprise Clark then brought up the subject of his marriage.

'I don't think I've been entirely fair to my wife.' This was said in a subdued voice, at least more subdued than before.

'What do you mean?'

'Well, I've always been more interested in money than anything else, to the extent that I've tended to push Holly on to the sidelines, almost out of my life. In fact I know I've been rather rude to her on many occasions. I've even forgotten her birthday and our anniversary, and other special occasions. I let Mabel handle all those things. And, yes, I've also been dismissive of our daughter and her new baby. It must have hurt Holly so much. I must try and make amends. I really must!' His final words did seem to carry conviction.

Smee knew very well what Clark was like with his family. Mabel had often told him about being responsible for the arrangements regarding birthdays and anniversaries. And, of course, he himself had occasionally been on the receiving end of his boss's lack of empathy. Indeed, many of his colleagues had discussed their boss's apparent unpleasantness with him. He decided to continue in this vein of conversation and perhaps get him to think about other areas where he might be kinder.

'What about the Ascalon charity? Will it go bankrupt along with the Keystones?'

'That's another thing,' said Clark. 'Why am I doing all this? We have the painting. It's worth a fortune. Do I really need the money? Certainly not. Keystone is really a very decent chap, and has done a lot to help others. I've never done any such thing – at least not in the same way as him. Perhaps I should not force this bankruptcy on his organisation. Perhaps I should bail them out. What do you think, Robert?'

Smee grabbed his chance with both hands. 'I think he should be saved. He's a good man and many others need him and his charity. Why not postpone the recall of the loan, sell the painting and use the money to help him out? After all, there might even be some good publicity for the bank in this. That wouldn't be a bad thing.'

'You're right. Yes, you're right!' exclaimed Clark.

This was music to Smee's ears. After all the years of having to endure his boss's coldly indifferent attitude to everything except money, he finally felt things were changing for the better. This was good. More whiskey was shared, and each tot went down ever more quickly. As it was now rather late in the evening, Smee made his excuses and went up to bed. Clark retired soon afterwards. They both had to be up early for breakfast and leave in good time for their 2.30pm flight from Cork to Heathrow. They were taking *The Lady in Green* with them and it had been arranged for them to be met at Heathrow by some of the

RPC Bank's security people, who would take charge of the painting.

The next morning they left Pelham House at nine and, with *The Lady in Green* securely packed in the boot, drove the seventy-odd miles to Cork airport, arriving in plenty of time for their flight. After checking in their baggage and entrusting the painting to the airport security team, they made their way to the nearest coffee shop in the departure lounge to await the flight to London. The time passed agreeably as they both recovered from the previous evening's slight overindulgence in whiskey. But no matter; the coffee they ordered was consumed with relish, followed by more cups, and the conversation tended to continue in the same vein as the night before.

A voice interrupted them.

'Hello, hello. Fancy meeting you here!'

Smee turned towards the voice, which was to his left. There stood a woman dressed in blue and white, with a nice smile and twinkling eyes. Next to her a man. Smee struggled for a second to recognise who she was, then he realised. It was the lady he had met on the ferry to Aranmore. Quite a coincidence.

'Hello! How nice to meet you again. Where are you going?'

'To London to meet friends. We decided to fly from Cork to meet my parents before flying off. They live in Cork and we stayed last night with them.' The woman spoke with a captivating accent and lovely smile. Clark decided to introduce himself, but was forestalled by Smee saying, 'This is my boss, Rupert Clark. We're both over here on business.' They shook hands with the woman.

Smee then said, 'It's Kathleen isn't it? I'm Robert Smee.'

'You've got a good memory, Robert! Yes. I'm Kathleen Delves-Broughton, but please call me Kathy. It's nice to meet you again. This is my husband, John. My, it's a small world isn't it?'

On this they all agreed. Clark invited Kathleen and John to join them for coffee. They had a pleasant hour talking together mostly about London and its environs. John Delves-Broughton knew London well, having worked there for many years as a manager in the National Health Service. Clark seemed to be enjoying the conversation, which again prompted Smee to realise how much this Irish adventure had changed his boss, who seemed much more outgoing and approachable; more readily prepared to listen not only to him but also, it would appear, to others. As though he'd undergone a complete change of heart in regard to life, money and family. If only this could be permanent!

'And your new grandson. What's he called? Have they picked a name for him yet?' Kathleen was very interested in babies. She told them proudly that she had three children and five grandchildren of her own, some of whom lived in and around London. Both she and her husband spent a great deal of time in the city, but were always glad to return to the peace, tranquillity and magnificent scenery of Aranmore. And, of course, they would often host their children and grandchildren for holidays on the island.

Clark said that no name had yet been chosen for his new grandson, but he was looking forward to seeing him for the first time when they got back to London.

The pleasant conversation between them was interrupted by the announcement over the public address system that gate seven was now boarding for the flight to London Heathrow.

There followed a general movement among the people surrounding them in the coffee bar as cabin luggage was collected and picked up and passengers made their way towards gate seven, which was at the far end of the departure lounge, but as they made their way there Clark continued the banter with Kathleen. He appeared to have really taken a shine to her, and didn't want their get-together to end. This was concluded while they were in the queue for boarding when Clark and Kathleen exchanged phone numbers. Clark promised to invite both Kathleen and John for lunch at Canary Wharf, when they were available, of course.

The four were not sitting near each other on the plane. Smee and Clark were at the rear of the cabin. Consequently Clark said goodbye to Kathleen and John as they boarded, thanking them for their friendliness and commenting upon Kathleen's lovely smile.

Kathleen looked at him, smiled even more and said, 'It's the only thing that you can give which is immediately returned with interest.'

'What's that?'

'A smile.'

The flight to London took an hour and twenty minutes, though they seemed to be hardly in the air before the aircraft started its descent. At Heathrow Smee and Clark were met by security people from the bank, who took charge of *The Lady in Green*, leaving them just to grab their luggage and make for the exit, where a car should be waiting to take them home. Smee was so looking forward to being with his wife and children. It had only been a few days away, yet it seemed so much longer because of all that had happened to him while in Ireland. He had such a story to tell.

Clark was also glad to be back home. He had not switched his phone on for the past four days and when he did so after reaching the main concourse of the airport, he was greeted by around 200 emails and 50-odd text messages. He made just one call, to his deputy, Spenlow, who was based at the bank's headquarters, and told him to deal with all his emails and anything else that had cropped up. For the time being he was going to forget work, be with his wife and visit his daughter and grandson.

It was Smee who spotted their driver first and pointed him out. As they approached him. Clark smiled at him and exchanged greetings. Soon they were in the car driving across London to Canary Wharf, where both had their own cars parked. They eventually reached their destination and the driver dropped them off in the car park. Clark's car was parked some way away from Smee's. They shook hands and parted, promising to meet the following Monday morning in the headquarters office. There they would discuss everything that had happened and decide the best way forward following on from all the events of the past week.

Clark sat in his car for a while and collected his thoughts. Would he ever recover from what had happened and be his old self? He thought not. This was to be the beginning of a new life for him and everyone around him. And with that firmly fixed in his mind, he headed for the M25 and home. His journey was soon over and he drew up outside his house and got out of the car. Almost immediately the front door opened and there, framed in the doorway, stood Holly, looking slightly apprehensive. She took a few steps towards him. He didn't walk towards her – he ran! And, sweeping the incredulous Holly off her feet, gave her a hug and a smile and a kiss. She was surprised, to say the least.

'Are you all right my dear?' she asked.

'Am I all right? You bet I am! I'm a very lucky chap indeed. I'm married to you. Please, please forgive all the rudeness and unkindness I've given you and that you've had to put up with all these years.'

Holly thought that the world was about to cave in. Nothing like this had happened to her for as long as she could remember. She was astonished. Had her husband gone mad?

'You look so nice when you smile,' was all she could think to say.

'It's the only thing that you can give which is immediately returned with interest.'

'What is?' asked Holly.

'A smile.'

Chapter 14

The weekend following Clark's return was spent mostly with his wife, daughter and new grandson, who had now been named William. Holly was overwhelmed by the difference in her husband. She had long ago given up expecting love, affection or anything like a normal married life with Rupert. Now he seemed to have become Mr Perfect: kind, considerate and thoughtful. She couldn't quite believe it. Their daughter, Hillary, was also stunned by the changes in her dad. The father she knew as an uncaring, work-focused grump had suddenly developed a different personality and become a man full of smiles and empathy. She thought the change was lovely. As for young William, it was not difficult to see that he was already the apple of his grandad's eye. For the first time in years the whole family spent a happy and joyous weekend together.

Smee's weekend was just as cheerful as that enjoyed by his boss. Again, he spent the whole time with Rosemary and their three children, mostly at home, though they did enjoy a little excursion to Central Park in Dartford, where they spent an afternoon enjoying the summer sunshine and lots of ice cream. Rosemary spent much of the rest of their time together listening to her husband talk about his experiences in Ireland, and even though his brush with the criminal element could have been a little off-putting, they decided that a holiday in Ireland would be a nice thing to do with the children. They began planning a trip for next year that would take them down the west coast of the Emerald Isle.

John Keystone had spent the day with Rita at their flat in Bristol. He had had discussions many times over the last few days with the estate agent in Ireland, who had told him a number of people were interested in their property, but only one had put in an offer and that was some €30,000 below the asking price. Conscious that the RPC Bank was demanding full payment of the loan without delay, they had decided to accept the offer. The money from the house sale, together with their savings and the little money from the sale of the paintings and other money from the sale of the contents of their Aranmore home, would pay off the bulk of the £407,000 that they owed. They had calculated that the amount still needed to fully pay off the loan was in the region of £20,000. This sum they had decided to borrow from a building society using their flat in Bristol as security. Keystone expected to have all the money together within two weeks. He could then pay off the loan and be free from, as he believed, the odious man who had hoodwinked him into taking the loan in the first place. This past week had been very difficult for both John and Rita, watching most of what they had built up over a period of many years threatened with collapse. Fortunately, they had not had to pull the plug immediately on the operation of their Ascalon charity. They had contacted three or four charity benefactors and explained the situation to them. Without exception, all had agreed to put some money towards maintaining the operation of the charity for the time being. Both John and Rita were very grateful for that.

Rita wanted to make one last visit to their home on Aranmore, not just to say, 'Goodbye,' to the house and neighbours, but also to collect some things of sentimental value from the contents and bring them back to their flat in Bristol. They would have to drive across to Ireland to do this, and use their large vehicle to bring the items back. They planned to do the trip the following week. John felt for Rita. She was more emotional than he was and she had shed more than a few tears as the full consequences of what was happening in their lives became apparent.

They were having a cup of tea when the phone rang. John was reading the newspaper and was particularly interested in the reports of the violent storms that had battered the Irish Atlantic coast over the previous few days. Wouldn't have wanted to have been at sea in that, he thought. Putting down his newspaper, he picked up the phone.

'Hello. John Keystone.'

'Good afternoon, Mr Keystone. My name is Johnson and I represent the RPC Bank.'

'What can I do for you?' asked Keystone.

'Well, Mr Clark was wondering whether you would be available to meet him at the bank's headquarters, tomorrow morning at eleven. Would that be possible, do you think?'

'What is the reason for this?'

'Oh, it's just that Mr Clark thinks he has something to say which may be of importance to you. Could you make the meeting please?'

Keystone really did not want to meet Clark ever again, but he was surprised by the phone call and the tone of the request. The chap at the other end was almost pleading with him to attend the meeting. He thought it would probably be a waste of time, but being such an amenable man, he replied, 'OK, I'll be there at eleven to meet him. Will anyone else be there?'

'There may be one or two others, but Mr Clark is looking forward to meeting you again.'

'I'm sure he is.' Keystone could not help the small degree of sarcasm that had crept into his voice with his last remark. He said goodbye and put the phone down.

'Who was that, darling?' asked Rita.

'Believe it or not, but it was the RPC Bank. It seems Rupert Clark would like to meet me tomorrow at the bank's head office to discuss something – the caller didn't say what. I'll have to catch an early train to make sure I get there in time.'

'Would you like me to come with you, darling?'

'Yes. That would be lovely! In fact, I'll introduce you to Clark and you can see for yourself what kind of a man he is. I'll phone and book the train tickets now.'

On Monday morning at ten past eight, Smee parked his car in the Canary Wharf Tower car park. He was in plenty of time for the meeting with his boss to consider a way forward from the present situation. He imagined this would be to discuss what to do with the painting of *The Lady in Green*, what to do about John Keystone and his debt to the RPC Bank, and any other related matters. His first contact was with Mabel who, looking up, gave him a warm welcome and asked how he had got on in Ireland.

'It was an experience I'll not forget,' he replied. 'In fact, I would love to tell you all about it, though we would need to put a couple of hours aside for me to get through all that happened while I was over there. It is a terrific place.'

Mabel said she would love to get together and hear all about it, and they agreed to meet for lunch in one of the many restaurants dotted around the area. Clark had not yet arrived, so Smee just sat in the chair near Mabel and told her some of his adventures of the past week, mentioning also the apparent change in their boss's personality. Mabel was intrigued. The conversation was interrupted by the arrival of Clark, who strode into the office full of bonhomie and with a smiling cheerful countenance.

'Good morning Mabel. And you Robert. Let's get the show on the road!' This kind of greeting from her boss was definitely not what Mabel was used to. She returned her boss's 'Good morning' and told him that Mr Spenlow would like a meeting as soon as convenient.

'Of course. I'll let you know just as soon as Robert and I have finished. But we have rather a lot to discuss, so we may be some time.'

'Righty-ho. I'll let him know that straight away.'

'Good. Now Robert, let's get inside and start work.'

Smee followed Clark into the inner office, where they both sat down at one of the tables. This was the office with the fabulous view across London that proved such a distraction to everyone who came there for the first time. It was possible to pick out most of the famous sights of the city: Tower Bridge, the London Eye, St Paul's Cathedral and the Shard. Even though Smee had been in here many times, he still found the panorama breathtaking. This office must surely rank among the most prestigious in the world, certainly with regard to its stupendous view. Little, he thought, could compare with it. It made him want to spend time just naming all the sights that could be seen!

'Yes, I know. It is terrific isn't it?' Clark had read Smee's thoughts from looking at his face. 'You know, I've never really appreciated this view. And you've given me an idea. My wife and daughter have never been here before. I really must invite them up for a look. I'm sure they would love it.'

Smee could only agree, and silently wished he could bring Rosemary and the children here. Perhaps he might suggest it to his boss later.

As though he'd read Smee's wish, Clark said, 'You should bring your family up here for a visit, Robert. I'm sure they'd like it too, although I guess I must be careful not to turn this office into a visitor attraction – that would never do!' This last remark was said with a faint smile on his lips and a sparkle in his voice.

'Crikey!' thought Smee, 'He's not just reading my mind, but making jokes about it now.'

John and Rita Keystone caught the seven o'clock train to Paddington. The train was very crowded, most people seeming to be commuters or travelling on business. Laptop computers were in evidence everywhere and the sound of keyboards being tapped filled the carriage with a kind of soft, dull music. John and Rita sat at a table for four, opposite a man and a woman fully engrossed in the screens in front of them who barely paused to look up. This state of affairs continued until the train stopped at Swindon, at which point Rita looked up from her newspaper and asked, 'Excuse me, but do you travel on this train every day?'

The question was directed at neither one nor the other but rather between the two, in the hope that one, or both, would provide an answer. The woman looked up from her laptop and was the first to reply.

'Well, not every day, but usually once or twice a week. My head office is in London you see and I often have to be there for meetings with staff or clients.'

'And what business are you in?' asked John, joining in with his wife in an attempt to get their two industrious companions chatting instead of focusing on their respective laptop keyboards.

'Banking. Investment banking. I work for the ITCD Bank.'

'I see. That must be interesting; all that travelling and spending time in London,' said Rita.

'Well, it can be, but it does take up a great deal of my time, at home and travelling, as you can see.'

The conversation attracted the attention of the man sitting opposite Rita and he joined in.

'We're both on the move most of the time. I also work in banking, for the KQ Freeman Bank in Canary Wharf. Jane and I are near neighbours in Bristol and try to travel together when we both have meetings in London. I'm Jack. Nice to meet you both.'

John and Rita reciprocated the greetings and introduced themselves. It was John who could not resist continuing the conversation by asking, 'Do you know the RPC Bank?'

Jane answered. 'Yes. I have had dealings with them on a few occasions. Do you know them?'

'Only slightly, through dealings with our charity, Ascalon.'

Jane, again. 'I know that charity. What's your connection with it?'

'My wife and I set it up some years ago and we still run it today.'

'My goodness, that must be quite a task! Running something so important to many people in Bristol. What made you decide to set it up?'

'Well, it's a long story. It was about eight years ago and we were visiting family in Bristol from our home in Ireland. It was in the winter, just around Christmas time, and very cold. We'd been to see a show with one of my sisters and had just left the theatre and were walking towards a taxi rank when we spotted a man huddled in a shop doorway. He looked in a bad way. We went to him and asked if there was anything we could do to help. He mumbled something about giving him some money, and it was when he looked up at us that I realised I knew him. He'd worked for me some years previously when I was running a construction company and he'd obviously fallen on hard times.'

Jane picked up on that. 'It was quite a coincidence, bumping into him like that. What did you do?'

'We offered him a bed for the night, but he refused. He only seemed interested in money then. Both Rita and

I tried to get him to come with us, but he kept repeating he didn't want to be a burden and asked could we give him a few pounds for some food. It was very sad. Eventually we gave him some money and arranged to meet him the following day and buy him lunch, which is what we did. He told us what had happened to him – how he'd lost his home after a divorce, then his job through redundancy, and continued on a downward spiral until he'd ended up where he was now.'

Rita added, 'Yes, he made both of us think just how fortunate we were to have each other and so much else. I think it was his sad story that made us decide to set up a charity to help others who found themselves in similar homeless situations. And that's what we did.'

Jack had been quiet while John and Rita told their story but now he joined in. 'Well, jolly well done to you both. What happened to the homeless man?'

John smiled as he recalled the story. 'Well, we managed to persuade him to stay in a nearby hostel that we funded, and through various contacts I had, he got a job working in the building trade. From there he was able to find a shared flat and become self-sufficient again. He still keeps in touch with us and he's doing well. We even had a contribution to our charity from him at Christmas time.'

'What a terrific story, and how many others have you helped get their lives back on track?'

'Oh, it must be hundreds and hundreds. Sometimes all that's needed is a little help at the right time.'

By now both Jack and Jane had closed their laptops and were engrossed in the story of the Ascalon charity. They were fulsome in their praise for both Rita and John, who of course, being typically British, were self-deprecating about what they had achieved.

John changed the subject back to what he was hoping might provide some information about the reason for their journey. 'But what do you know about the RPC Bank? I understand it's quite successful.' He wasn't adept at fishing for information, but he thought he would give it a try anyway, while the opportunity was there of having two bankers in conversation. Rita knew exactly what he was trying to do, and she too was hoping for a response from the pair sitting opposite.

Jack replied, 'Well, they're not a very big bank and were set up only a few years ago, so they are really new boys in the investment banking game. I've had dealings with them and they seem to be pretty switched on. Their boss has quite a reputation.'

'Oh yes. Is he one of these City financial wizards?'

'Not too sure about that. But he has pulled off some interesting deals.'

'Interesting? In what ways?'

'Well, all completely legal and above board of course, but he has quite a reputation for ruthlessness.'

Jane took up the exchange. 'And, I'm told,' she said, 'that he is focused so much on the success of his bank that nothing, absolutely nothing, is allowed to get in his way, including his family.'

'Oh dear, how very sad for them,' commented Rita.

The four of them continued their conversation around charity work in Bristol, banking and the state of the nation. They shared coffee and biscuits as the train sped its way through the Berkshire countryside towards Paddington.

John and Rita had planned to use the underground to get to Canary Wharf but Jack and Jane insisted they shared a black cab ride to their common destination instead. They accepted the offer and the four of them continued their journey towards those modern skyscrapers that form an integral part of the London skyline.

'What are we going to do with the painting of the lady in green?' Clark's question, put to Smee, had an air of casualness about it, as if it really didn't matter at all.

'Probably best to sell it as soon as possible, and use the money for something else,' was Smee's response.

'Yes. Good idea. Let's do just that. Get Sotheby's on the phone and they can announce its sale soon.'

Smee did so. The auction house's response to the description of the painting and its painter, and the fact that its provenance had been confirmed by Henderson, was to ask where the painting was stored, so they could send their people to view it and take pictures for inclusion in an auction catalogue. Smee gave them the name of the bank that had the painting in its vaults. He then rang the bank and told them to expect visitors from Sotheby's.

In the black cab, the journey to Canary Wharf took around twenty minutes. When they arrived, the four new friends thanked each other and wished each a successful day. John and Rita had arrived in plenty of time for their meeting. It was Rita's first visit to Canary Wharf and she was struck with awe on seeing the Tower for the first time.

'What a magnificent building! Tremendous!' she said.

'Yes,' replied John. 'If only some of the people inside it were as magnificent.'

They walked towards the entrance slowly, mainly because Rita kept stopping to look about at all the other sights and buildings in the area. Eventually they reached the main entrance. John took Rita to one of the many lifts on the ground floor, where they joined a small queue waiting to enter. Once inside they made slow progress, for the lift made many stops on the way to the forty-ninth floor and the offices of RPC Bank. They walked into the outer office and John went up to Mabel's desk and introduced them. Mabel recognised Keystone from his previous visit and, after asking them both if they had a nice journey, said, 'Of course. I'll let Mr Clark know you're here.'

Mabel suggested that they both sit down to wait however there was not enough time for this as the speaker on her desk said, 'Please show them in.' John recognised the voice immediately.

Mabel opened the inner office door for them. As they entered Clark's office Rita was apprehensive, John resigned.

'Please sit down. And Mrs Keystone, so nice to meet you at last. I'm Rupert Clark and this is my senior aide, Robert Smee.' Both offered their hands to Rita, who willingly accepted them. Once John and Rita were seated comfortably, John said, 'Please could you tell us why we have been asked here? Is it anything to do with reducing the loan repayment period?'

Clark beamed at them. 'No. Certainly not. In fact I have a proposition to put to you that is quite the opposite. You see, I've just returned from Ireland where the paintings you sold me have been valued by an art expert. He has suggested that one of them may well be worth a considerable sum. He believes the painting of the lady in green to be by Sir Joshua Reynolds. And this has been confirmed by other experts. It is my wish that you have the painting as a gift from me and use the money it generates to repay the loan and help with the work of your charity. How does that sound?'

John Keystone sat open-mouthed, struggling to comprehend what had just been said. Rita was thinking that Clark seemed a decent man and not at all like the mean-spirited, grasping and Scrooge-like individual that John had previously described. There were a few seconds of silence before John said, 'Are you serious?'

'I most certainly am. Please accept my offer.'

'Of course. Of course! Yes! This is wonderful! Thank you. Thank you.'

'Good. Now we have taken the liberty of contacting Sotheby's in London. They are prepared to auction the painting at their next sale, which is to be held in late September. Provided you are OK with this we can press the button and the sale will go ahead. Is that OK?'

Still struggling to take all this in, John said, 'Absolutely!'

'Good. Then it shall be done.' Clark nodded towards Smee, who left the office to contact Sotheby's and tell them to go ahead with the sale.

'Now, would you like some coffee? Black or white?'

'Oh, white please,' the pair said simultaneously, and almost instantly Mabel brought in a tray of coffee accompanied by some very tasty-looking biscuits. John was still struggling to get over the shock caused by this apparent turnaround. He needed to find out what had caused it.

'This is very generous of you, but is there any particular

reason for this, may I say, unexpected offer? It has been quite a shock.'

'I quite understand why you would say that. Let's just say that I've been reminded very much recently that life is not just about money and the single-minded pursuit of wealth. And perhaps I've spent too much time thinking and acting as if it were all about those things. I'm glad to say that now I appreciate the more important things in life.'

Rita had spent most of the last few minutes listening to this astounding conversation. She found it fascinating and, of course, was relieved and delighted that any money coming from the sale of the painting would mean the charity was safe. She prayed that it would not be too late to prevent the sale of their beloved home on Aranmore going through. Her thoughts were in something of a turmoil; after all that she had been told by John, after all that had happened over the last few weeks, especially seeing John become more and more miserable, suddenly all was sweetness and light! She felt ecstatic. After they had finished drinking their coffee, Rita could not resist asking Clark one question.

'Mr Clark, I must say you are very fortunate to work in an office with such fabulous views. How on earth do you manage to concentrate to do any work?'

'Do you know, surprisingly, I never took much notice until very recently! The London skyline is rather special though, isn't it?'

Now the business was out of the way and the atmosphere was friendlier than it had been the last time John Keystone was in this office, the conversation became easier and more sociable between the four of them until the time came for the Keystones to leave in order to catch their train back to Bristol.

'Please come up to London for the auction of the painting. Lunch afterwards will be on me. I'll let you know the date,' said Clark.

'We will definitely join you for that. Looking forward to it!' said Rita.

John and Rita took the lift nearest the office. It was empty, so John immediately embraced his wife and together they gave thanks for the completely unexpected salvation that had been delivered to them and the charity. For John, the journey in the lift to the ground floor was considerably different from the last time he had to take it. He thought that whatever had brought on the change in Clark's personality must have been something of quite staggering magnitude. A miracle, no less.

Chapter 15

The auction room at Sotheby's in New Bond Street, London, was crowded. John and Rita Keystone, as the owners of an item to be auctioned, had been allocated reserved seats near the front along with and next to Rupert Clark and his wife, Holly. It was two months since their last meeting in Canary Wharf and much had happened in that time. Ascalon had been rescued from possible collapse by Clark's generous donation. Now, they hoped, the painting of the lady in green would fetch a very good price and further contribute to the funds of the charity. Both Rita and John were filled with warm expectation. There were other items for sale that day and it was some time before the *Lady in Green* made her appearance.

No doubt the packed auction room was due in large measure to the publicity given to the painting through the press and media. The fascinating story behind its discovery and journey in Ireland had lent it a certain notoriety in the art world. The fact that it was by Sir Joshua Reynolds was likely to guarantee it a place among the top works of art for sale anywhere in the world for some time. Needless to say, the story of the painting's discovery and perilous journey contained no account of the less than generous part played by Rupert Clark. This had been glossed over. He had by now become a supporting figure in the whole story, though an important one.

The auctioneer announced the next lot. 'And now, a recently discovered work by the great eighteenth-century artist, Sir Joshua Reynolds. The painting is of a lady in green. The sitter is unknown, though could possibly be Nelly O'Brien, of whom it is said Reynolds was very fond.'

While the auctioneer made this short introduction, two white-gloved men carried the painting into the auction room and mounted it on a stand for all to see. The effect could be felt quite clearly. The audience in the room was transfixed by the painting. Indeed, Smee, who had secured a seat at the back of the room, felt the same as he had when he first encountered it all those weeks ago on Aranmore. The look from the face and eyes of the lady in the painting stopped most people in their thoughts and provoked a question. This question would mostly be, 'How did Reynolds paint that look?' or 'Any woman who could fix you with a look like that would surely rule the world'. Once the painting was secure in position the auctioneer continued.

'Lot 555, a recently discovered work by Sir Joshua Reynolds of a lady in green. There is a reserve price for this painting. Would someone open the bidding at two million pounds?'

Rita gulped. A hand went up near the front, quickly followed by a succession of discreet hand movements around the room. The bidding soon reached four million, going up in increments of a hundred thousand. It was then that the four people seated at the long desk at the side of the auction room, all of whom were holding phones to their ears, entered the bidding process. The atmosphere became increasingly intense, and when the bid reached five and a half million, Rita and John gripped hands tightly in disbelief and comforting reassurance. How could this painting that they had bought along with their house on Aranmore be worth so much?

The auctioneer seemed to become calmer and more measured the higher the bidding figure reached. In fact his voice had slowed to a crawl, and John Keystone thought that if the bids went much higher, the auctioneer would be speaking so slowly he might fall asleep.

'I have one bid at five million seven hundred pounds on the telephone. Is there any advance on five million seven hundred pounds?'

In the auction room there was silence for a few seconds, then a man's voice near the front of the room said 'Six million', accompanied by a wave of his hand, which was holding a white card inscribed with a number. Rita gasped and thought surely that must be it. Surely!

'I am bid six million pounds. Any advance on that sum. Have you all done?'

There were shaking heads from the telephone operators at the side, and continued silence from the other bidders in the room.

Rita gulped again.

'Going once...going twice...at six million pounds. All done?' Silence.

'Sold!' and the auctioneer's gavel came down hard on his sounding block.

The auction room erupted in spontaneous applause

and John and Rita embraced. Clark shook hands with John and Smee came forward from the back of the room to join in the handshakes and backslapping.

John, clutching Rita closely to his chest, said, 'Darling, our charity is saved and we can go on to greater things. This is a real turning point. Is it really true?'

'Yes it is, my love, though it's hard to believe considering all that's happened over the past few months!' It had been quite a day!

Clark was more than pleased with the outcome. He gathered John, Rita and Smee together and said, 'Well done, all. What a brilliant result! Now we must celebrate. Please, you must all join me for lunch. I know a nice little restaurant in Maiden Lane, not far from here. I have booked a table and we can walk there easily if you are all OK with that.' They all agreed.

There were many people outside Sotheby's and their walk to the restaurant was slow to start as they negotiated the crowds of people outside the auction house. Clark suddenly shouted to someone in front of him, 'William! It's William Wolf, isn't it?'

And it was. William turned towards Clark and said, 'Hello. Nice to see you again.'

'What are you doing here, so far from home?'

'I live here now. I've got a place at King's College studying ancient history and philosophy. I thought I'd come along to the auction to see what price the painting would fetch.'

'Well done on your placement,' said Clark, who then introduced William to the Keystones.

'This is William. We shared the experience along the

west coast of Ireland together. One I'll never forget, and I don't imagine you will either, William.'

'No, sir,' said William.

'Would you like to join us for lunch? My treat! The restaurant is only a short walk away,' said Clark.

'Would love to,' replied William.

And that is how Rita, John, Clark, Smee and William came to dine at the rather nice restaurant in Maiden Lane, where they discussed the whole fabulous story of *The Lady in Green*, the countryside and drinking places of Ireland, the voyage of the good ship *An Luchog* and her crew of diverse personalities, the raging storm that so nearly cost the lives of those on board, the hundredth birthday of Patrick Lewington in Doolin and, after Clark had consumed a couple of glasses of wine, the appearance and disappearance of the stowaway, Michael.

The lunch lasted well into the afternoon and was certainly very celebratory. Everyone was enjoying themselves and no one seemed to want it to end.

The first to leave were Rita and John Keystone. They had not planned to stay in London overnight and set off to catch the train back to Bristol, saying goodbye to all as they left and got a taxi to Paddington station.

William was thoroughly enjoying himself. He was still not entirely keen on alcohol, despite now being a university student, and confined himself to drinking lime and soda, but the food was delicious – all three courses. It made a wonderful change from the food he was used to eating in his student digs, which consisted mostly of beans on toast and the occasional fast-food beef burger and chips! Clark kept asking him questions about Michael, which he could not answer. The how, when and where of this questioning was persistent and tiring, but William kept up an attentive front while enjoying the food on offer. Smee was also having a great time and was glad of the opportunity to get to know William. The last time they had met was in the Eastend pub in Fenit, when the crew of *An Luchog* were celebrating their survival. William told Smee how surprised and pleased he'd been when his exam results had been good enough to allow him to secure a place at King's College reading the subjects he'd wanted to study, and Smee said, 'Well, you must be very pleased with your results – and what an opportunity, to study here in London. You're very fortunate.'

William agreed and asked Smee what he would be doing in the future. Before he could answer, Clark, who had had an ear open for their conversation, cut in. 'He's going to continue working for me. And he's going to get a big pay rise. Aren't you Robert? Job done.'

Robert Smee had lost count of the number of surprises he had experienced over the last few months. This was another one, certainly the best surprise he'd ever had.

'Well, yes, of course. Looking forward to it.'

Clark looked at William and said, 'And when you are ready, my lad, if you would like to, please come and see me about how you might fit in to my organisation. I'm sure we can find something to keep you busy. By the way, how are the crew of *An Luchog*? Do you have any contact with them?'

'I do,' said William. 'I sailed with them until my exam results came through. We navigated around most of Ireland transporting different goods. It was good experience. I'm still in contact with Kazi by email. He lets me know, when he can, where they are and what they're doing. I do miss the times I spent with them. But being a student in London does have its advantages.'

By now it was approaching four o'clock and their meal was over. William was the next to leave, promising to keep in touch with both of them.

Clark and Smee got up from their table and headed towards the door. There were just a few diners left in the restaurant now. They stepped into Maiden Lane and began walking down a narrow street towards the Strand, where Clark had suggested would be the best place to get a taxi back to Canary Wharf. As they went past the stage door of the Adelphi Theatre, which opened on to the narrow street, the door opened and a man dressed in the most bizarre costume imaginable came out. The costume was full-length with a winged cape at the back and was of an incredible array of colours – a technicolour coat in fact. To Smee, this was obviously one of the performers in whatever show was on at the moment, though what type of show it was he was not exactly sure. The coat of many colours, however, was a bit of a giveaway.

Clark had stopped dead and stood open-mouthed before exclaiming, 'Michael, Michael! It's you, by all that's holy, it's Michael!' His voice was jubilant.

Smee stopped too and looked at the outlandishly dressed figure in front of him. Could this be the man his boss kept going on and on about? Well, judging by Clark's reaction it certainly would seem so.

'It is you! It is! Give me your hand.' Clark had already grabbed Michael's hand and was shaking it furiously.

'Where have you been and what are you doing here? Thank you again and again. Thank you for all you did to save us. And thank you for changing my life! Goodness me, are you actually appearing in this show?'

Michael looked at them both and said, 'Hello, Mr Clark. Fancy seeing you here of all places. Yes I'm in the show, and enjoying it. I shall be in it until next week. It's a great show.'

'But how? Where did you disappear to after we had our chat outside the pub in Fenit? You seemed to vanish into thin air.'

'Oh, I thought I'd mentioned to you that I had to get to Malin Head quickly. There was another boat in difficulties there. Thankfully all that is resolved now, and as a reward, I've been given this chance to perform here at this theatre.'

'I'll have to come and see you, and bring my family.'

'Well, the box office is selling tickets at the front of the theatre.'

'I'll get some now. But tell me, how does someone get to be on a boat in the Atlantic off the west coast of Ireland one day, and then just a few weeks later get to be performing at the Adelphi in London? And what did you have to do at Malin Head? Sounds as if you're at it non-stop!'

'It's all the boss's responsibility,' said Michael. 'He tells me where to go and what to do. I just love being under his leadership. He's told me that having this performing experience will help me to appreciate people better and give me a greater understanding of life.'

'Has he got an office?' asked Smee, who had been listening with interest to the conversation, and was wondering what kind of boss gives his employees such varied opportunities and experiences.

'Of course he has an office. In fact he has offices just about everywhere,' replied Michael.

'What kind of company does he run and what sort of business is it in? Is it a global outfit?' Smee's questions tumbled from him in a torrent.

'Sure is. Very global. Actually, universal.' An acute observer would have noticed Michael confined himself to answering Smee's last question only.

Just then the stage door opened and a young lady dressed in a similarly colourful outfit to Michael, and obviously a cast member, stuck her head around the door and, looking at Michael, said, 'Michael, please come quickly. We are starting again now. We're all waiting for you.'

'OK Gillian, I'll be with you now.' Michael then turned to Clark and Smee and said, 'Must go. Hope you manage to get tickets to the show,' and he turned towards the stage door. Even as Michael was almost through the door, Clark could not resist one more question.

'Where does your boss live? I'd love to meet him.'

'Oh, he's everywhere. Try St Mary's church in the Strand. It's quite near here. Sit at the front and pray. You would get very close to him there.' The stage door closed.

Author's Note

The inspirations for this novel were many and varied. My thanks especially, to the 1950s Ealing film comedy *The Maggie*, to the 1940s films *It's a Wonderful Life* and *The Bishop's Wife*, and an anonymous and wonderful couple for permission to use their fabulous painting of the lady in green (artist unknown). My special thanks of course, go to my wife, Deb, for all her support and encouragement. And just in case you are wondering, '*an luchog*' is Irish Gaelic for 'the mouse'.